Control All Delete

Exposing the Elite's Agenda

H. K. Frontier

Critical Brains
DARE TO KNOW

Contents

Chapter 1

Kin and Kismet

Valhalla District is a city built on silence and fear. Its towering metallic structures stretch endlessly upward, blotting out the sky. Their surfaces reflect the artificial light that keeps the streets in a state of perpetual twilight. The stars have long been forgotten here, and even the sun seems like a distant memory, obscured by the ever-present smog that hangs thick in the air.

Alex Vanguard walks the streets with his head down, moving with a mechanical efficiency that's become second nature. The people around him—if they can even be called people anymore—move in much the same way, eyes fixed on the ground, shoulders hunched, their steps hurried and purposeful. No one makes eye contact. No one speaks. In Valhalla District, silence is survival.

The air smells like a marbling of burnt metal and the antiseptic used in hospitals. It's a smell Alex has grown used to, though he doesn't remember when. In Valhalla, you either adapt or you disappear.

A drone's shadow flits across his path, and he resists the urge to look up. They're always there anyway, their metallic bodies glinting in the dull light as they patrol in precise patterns, red eyes scanning the streets below. If only they were as good at weather control as they were at surveillance—Valhalla could use some actual sunshine.

Always watching and always recording, they're equipped with cutting-edge facial recognition and gait recognition. The state's control is absolute, and the drones are its eyes and ears.

Alex passes by a kiosk, its neon lights flickering slightly as it advertises the day's meal "options." They're all pretty much the same, but the illusion of choice is one of the state's most effective misdirects.

There's nothing appetizing about the choices displayed on the screen—just the same synthetic, nutrient-packed food that's been keeping the population alive for years. Real food—the kind that grows from the earth, that has flavor and texture—is a luxury reserved for the elites. The rest of the population must survive on these lifeless imitations.

With a sigh, Alex orders a burger. The machine inside the kiosk whirs to life as it assembles the meal with clinical precision. It's a process that's become so routine, so automated, that Alex barely notices it anymore. He swipes his wrist across the payment scanner, feeling the slight vibration as the Central Bank Digital Currency (CBDC) deducts from his account. Another meaningless transaction in a city where nothing feels real anymore.

The burger is warm in his hands, but that's about the only good thing Alex can say about it. As he takes a bite, the familiar taste—or lack thereof—fills his mouth. It's almost impressive how it manages to be both soggy and dry at the same time, but it does its job: it fills the void in his stomach. Like everything else, it operates out of pure functionality.

He chews slowly, his thoughts drifting as he makes his way through the streets, each step carrying him closer to home. The city around him feels like it's closing in, the tall buildings looming over him like silent sentinels. These identical high-rises, where the GSF houses everyone in state-controlled apartments, stretch endlessly toward the sky. Every corner is monitored, every street watched by the ever-present surveillance systems that have become so deeply ingrained in the fabric of society. There's no escaping it. Valhalla District is a cage; everyone in it is a prisoner.

But as Alex discovered years ago, people don't realize that they're locked in a cage until the key has turned in the lock.

As Alex reaches his apartment building, a device scans his retinal ID before allowing him entry, and the door slides open. The inside is as cold and sterile as the streets outside. The walls are bare, the floors polished to a mirror-like shine. It's efficient, functional, and devoid of any warmth or personality. Just like everything else in this city.

Inside his apartment, the automatic lights turn on as he steps through the door. The space is quiet—too quiet, almost—and the only sound is the soft hum of the air filtration system. Much like the city outside, the apartment feels more like a machine than a home.

Mila is in the kitchen with her back to him, her petite frame silhouetted against the holographic interface. Her dark hair is pulled back in its usual perfect bun, not a strand out of place—exactly how the Global Safety Foundation likes its citizens to appear. Her fingers move rapidly across the floating display as she works on some project or other. She doesn't look up.

"Dinner's almost ready," she says, her voice flat, emotionless.

"I already ate," Alex mutters, tossing the remains of the synthetic burger onto the counter. "It doesn't matter anyway. All the food tastes the same."

Mila pauses, her fingers hovering over the hologram before she resumes her work. She doesn't respond, but Alex can feel the disappointment radiating from her. It's been like this for a while now—this distance between them, this disconnect. They used to be close, back when the world still made sense. But that was *before*. Before the world turned into this cold, controlled place. Before everything became automated, synthetic, and soulless.

His eyes drift to the violin hanging on the wall, the polished wood gleaming in the dim light. It's the only decoration in the apartment and the only reminder of the life they used to have. Mila used to play every night. Her music filled the air with warmth and life. But now, the violin is just a decoration, a relic of a time that feels distant and unreachable.

Alex sinks onto the couch, running a hand through his hair as he lets out a tired sigh. His body aches—not from any physical exertion, but from the mental and emotional exhaustion that comes with living in a world where everything feels like a struggle. His job drains him daily, with each hour spent maintaining the very systems that keep everyone in line, including himself.

Mila steps into the living room, wiping her hands on a towel as she watches him from the doorway. "You could've waited," she says quietly. Her voice is soft but edged with frustration. "It would've been nice to have dinner together."

Alex shrugs, his eyes still fixed on the violin. "Sorry. I was starving."

She doesn't respond immediately; she just stands there, watching him with that same look of disappointment she's had for months now. "It's not about the food, Alex," she says finally. "It's about us. We don't even spend time together anymore."

"I'm here, aren't I?" Alex replies, though he knows how hollow the words sound even as he says them.

Mila shakes her head, turning away from him. "Sometimes it feels like you're not."

She walks back into the kitchen, leaving Alex alone with his thoughts. He leans his head back against the couch, closing his eyes as he lets out another sigh. He knows she's right. They've grown more and more distant, both lost in their own worlds.

But what can he do? In Valhalla District, there's no room for real connections, no room for anything that makes life worthwhile or evokes true emotion. Everything is designed to keep people alive, not to let them truly live.

His wrist communicator buzzes, pulling him from his thoughts. He glances down at the screen: *Mom and Dad's 50th Anniversary Tomorrow. Write Note.*

Alex stares blankly at the notification, and a wave of guilt washes over him. He would've forgotten. It's been so long since he's seen his parents, so long since they've spoken beyond the occasional (monitored) message. They live far outside the city, in one of the rural provinces where the denizens are monitored, but life is a little easier. The folks out there aren't considered potential threats—they don't have any fight left in them.

"You should call them," Mila says from the kitchen, her voice softer now, almost gentle. "It's been a while." She would have received the same anniversary notification.

"I will," Alex lies, knowing full well that he won't. He doesn't have the energy for a phone call, doesn't have the words. What would he even say? Everything feels so...disconnected. Even his parents are like strangers now, any ties that held them together torn to shreds by the system.

Instead of calling, he taps the screen of his wrist communicator, activating the AI assistant. "Compose a message," he mutters.

The AI initializes, and its digital voice is smooth and soothing. "Please provide the recipient's name and the message you'd like to send."

"Parents. Anniversary message," Alex says, leaning back against the couch as the AI begins drafting the message for him. The words appear on the screen, neat and tidy, perfectly polite but devoid of real emotion:

Dear Mom and Dad, Happy Anniversary! I wish I could be there to celebrate with you. It's been so long. Have a wonderful day!

He doesn't bother reading the rest. It's a nice enough message, polite and well-structured, but those aren't his words. He may as well have just signed his name on a card. He approves the message, letting the AI send it off with a tap of the screen. Task complete. One more thing off the list.

Mila steps into the living room, her brow furrowed slightly. "You didn't even write it yourself?"

Alex shrugs, feeling the weight of exhaustion pressing down on him. "So what? It's all the same, isn't it?"

Mila sighs, shaking her head as she walks back into the kitchen. But she doesn't push. She never pushes.

The silence that follows her departure feels heavier than usual, though, like there's something between them that neither wants to confront. Alex sits there, staring at the empty space where Mila had stood, his mind drifting as the minutes tick by.

He knows something needs to change, but in Valhalla District, change feels like a distant dream. Every day is the same. Every interaction, every task, every thought—controlled, monitored, regulated. He doesn't even know who he is anymore. Just another cog in the machine.

He does know that he used to have dreams. These days, Conformity Corp ensures that a dream remains just that; only the elites have the resources to make them come true. They control everything: who gets to eat real food, who can travel outside the city, who lives free from constant surveillance, and who gets to make their own choices.

The mechanical whisper of the air filtration system reminds him that even the air they breathe isn't really theirs. The air is owned, controlled, and distributed. They don't own anything anymore—not their homes, food, or even the air in their lungs. True freedom is a distant memory—something fossilized that will never be excavated.

Alex's gaze drifts toward Jackson's room, where a blue glow flickers beneath the door—the holographic boundary projected by his son's VR system. He hasn't seen his son since the previous night, and the realization makes his heart hurt.

"Jackson's still in his room?" Alex asks.

"Where else?" Mila replies from the kitchen, her voice flat and tired. "He's in Bali this time, I think. Or maybe a fancy resort on Mars? I can't keep track."

Alex doesn't respond. He knows it's not worth asking more. Like so many in this city, his son has chosen to escape into the virtual world rather than face the reality of this life. It is hard to blame his son; it is hard to blame any of them.

Jackson's body may be here, but his mind is perpetually elsewhere, lost in the endless possibilities of escaping to virtual worlds—most of the time, Jackson is like the fifth wall in a room.

The propaganda channel on the wall screen continues its relentless broadcast, the voice of President Kleton filling the room with empty promises and talk of progress, safety, and unity. It's all lies, of course. The city isn't thriving; it's barely surviving. But no one would dare say that out loud.

The president's words are meant to comfort and reassure, but Alex feels nothing but indifference as the message repeats itself, a broken record of lazy but well-crafted promises. He knows better. Everyone in Valhalla District knows better but is too afraid to admit it, too afraid to speak out, to push back, and even to think about resisting.

Alex's wrist communicator buzzes again, pulling him from his thoughts. This time, it's a notification from his employer, UmbraCorp, reminding him of the tasks he needs to complete before the end of the week. He swipes it away, not wanting to think about work. Not tonight.

He leans back on the couch, closing his eyes. The city outside drones on with its life—a word that's become something of a euphemism—and Alex can feel the world closing in around him, tightening its grip.

Suffocating him.

This is all by design, of course: the less he can breathe, the less he can think; the less he can think, the less he can change anything. Change is a threat to the system.

His system.

There was a time when Alex believed in the power of technology, when his hands flew across keyboards with purpose and pride, engineering the future. He remembers the excitement in those early days, the burning conviction that AI would liberate humanity from its limitations. He remembers drawing up the blueprints for the very systems that now monitor every breath, track every transaction, and control every aspect of life in Valhalla District.

He built this prison. Line by line of code, innovation by innovation, all while telling himself he was creating paradise.

The irony threatens to choke him. His algorithms, originally designed to enhance human potential, now suppress it. His AI systems, meant to serve humanity, have become its masters. Every drone that hovers overhead, every surveillance camera that tracks movement, every digital currency transaction that leaves its permanent mark—they all carry pieces of his work within them.

What can one person do against such a monster?

The guilt gnaws at him constantly, like a cancer eating away at his conscience. He sees it in every blank stare from the citizens of Valhalla District and in every mindless interaction with the machines that govern their lives. His innovations, twisted and perverted, have helped forge the chains that bind them all.

Alex once thought that technology could be the key to a brighter future. Now, he knows better, but it's too late. The system is too powerful. His creation has outgrown its creator, and he's as much its prisoner as anyone else.

He opens his eyes, his gaze again landing on Mila's violin. She was once a super-talented musician with a bright future. Her beautiful music was something of a soundtrack for their lives. He imagines what it would be like if she picked it up again, if the apartment were filled with music instead of silence. But that's not their life anymore. That part of them—of her—is gone.

"Alex?" Mila's voice startles him from his thoughts. She's standing in the doorway again, frowning with her arms crossed. "You all right?"

"I'm good. Just tired."

Mila watches him for a moment, her eyes searching his face for something, but whatever she's looking for, she doesn't find it. She starts rubbing her temples as if fighting off exhaustion. But that's not what this is, and Alex knows it.

"You've been so distant lately," she says quietly, her voice softening. "More than usual. Is it just work? Or is something else going on?"

"Nothing important," Alex says. "Just the usual. You know...life."

Mila purses her lips and nods, the silence between them growing heavier. After a few beats, she turns and walks back into the kitchen, leaving Alex alone with his thoughts once more.

He doesn't know how much longer he can live like this. Every day feels like a battle, not just with the system but with himself. A battle to keep going and pretend that everything is fine when it's anything but.

The sound of Jackson's laughter filters through his bedroom door, the sound tinny and distant, as though it's coming from some other world, far away from this one. Of course, in a way, it is.

Alex stands up from the couch, shakes the stiffness from his legs, and walks over to Jackson's door. He stops for a moment before knocking lightly. There's no response, but he didn't expect one. Jackson is too far gone in his virtual world to notice.

"Jackson?" Alex calls out, knocking again. "Can I come in, bud?"

No reply. No recognition.

Alex pushes the door open. His son is lying on his bed, the VR headset firmly in place, his body still as his mind wanders through some distant digital landscape.

For a few seconds, Alex just watches him, a marbling of sadness and frustration filling his chest. This isn't how things were supposed to be. Jackson should be out in the world, living, experiencing life, being a teenager.

Hell, Alex remembers when he was that age and the harmless trouble he'd get into as he was finding his way in the world. He hadn't had the choice to escape into some virtual world where nothing from reality could hurt him. Would he have taken that route? He doesn't think so. But who's to say? Regardless, Jackson has definitively chosen to escape into the virtual, just like so many others.

"Jackson!" Alex says again, this time with the volume turned up. He steps closer and places a hand on his son's shoulder, gently shaking him as if waking the boy from a dream.

Jackson flinches, startled, and jolts up. He pulls off the headset, blinking in confusion as he looks up at his father. "Dad? What the hell? Ever hear of knocking?"

"I did," Alex says. "A few times."

"Okay, well, what's so important?"

"I just wanted to talk," Alex says. "You've been in here for hours."

Jackson sighs and rubs his eyes. "Yeah, I guess I lost track of time. It's easy to do."

Alex can't argue with that. It *is* easy to lose track of time. And it's not as though Jackson's missing out on all that much.

Alex sits on the edge of the bed. "Where were you this time? Japan? Jupiter?"

"The Maldives," Jackson says, a small smile tugging at the corner of his lips. "It was insane. The clear water, the white beaches, it was all so...real."

Alex nods, though he doesn't know what to say. How can he argue with that? In a world as cold and controlled as theirs, who wouldn't want to escape into something beautiful, even if it's *not* actually real?

"You should come out for dinner," Alex says, though he knows it's a futile request. "Your mom synthesized something."

Jackson shakes his head. "I'm good."

"Jackson—"

"Dad, I'm fine," Jackson interrupts. "Just let me be, okay? I'm not hungry."

Alex opens his mouth to argue, but the words die on his lips. There's no point. Jackson is too far gone, too deep in his virtual world to care about anything else.

With a heavy sigh, Alex stands up and walks toward the door. "Okay," he says quietly. "I'll leave you to it. Have fun."

Jackson doesn't reply—he's already pulled the VR headset back over his eyes, disappearing once again into his digital paradise.

As Alex steps out into the hallway, closing the door softly behind him, the quiet once again makes him miss something he can't quite put his finger on. The drones, the surveillance, the synthetic food, the AI-generated messages, the propaganda machines—it's all just white noise, drowning out anything real or organic.

He walks back to the living room, sinking onto the couch. Outside, the drones continue their endless patrols, their red lights unblinking like artificial stars in a sky that no longer remembers what real stars look like.

Alex closes his eyes, the exhaustion pulling at him, dragging him down into the heavy, suffocating quiet of the night. He wonders—and not for the first or last time—if his subconscious is the only place where his dreams can still safely reside.

Chapter 2

Art and Artifice

Alex's mornings are a treadmill of routine and ritual. The system knows exactly when he's supposed to rise and be productive—it's the system he helped perfect. These days, he wakes even before the automated lights detect his movement and flood the room with their artificial glow.

Today feels no different than any other day. The sterile light floods the room as the blinds retract automatically, revealing a grey sky over Valhalla Center. The massive towers of UmbraCorp and other giant corporations fill the horizon. Their surfaces gleam with the artificial intelligence he proudly helped integrate into their networks.

From the moment Alex's eyes open, he knows what the day holds—a monotonous grind through a job that has long since lost its purpose. The spark of innovation that once

drove him to create "revolutionary" monitoring systems has been smothered by witnessing how those same systems now strangle society's every breath.

He slides out of bed, moving through the motions without thought. Shower, dress, and out the door. His reflection stares back at him from the bathroom mirror—dark hair graying at the temples and tired brown eyes with deepening shadows beneath them. The face of a man who helped build his own prison.

His wardrobe consists of the same bland corporate attire, interchangeable and unremarkable. Personal expression is disallowed; once it reaches a certain level, it's illegal. The Conformity Corps monitors everything from clothing choices to social media posts, flagging any deviation from approved patterns as potential dissidence. Standing out means being noticed, and being noticed means being watched more closely. Efficiency is the only value left that's worth anything to the system—a mantra he once preached in boardrooms, never imagining how it would suffocate humanity's spirit.

The elevator ride down to the street level is as uneventful as it is brief. A few neighbors stand beside him, silent, eyes locked on the notifications flashing on their wrist communicators. No one speaks anymore, not unless it's necessary. Alex recognizes the social analytics algorithm running on their devices—his early work on behavioral modification twisted into a tool for enforcing silence.

He used to try making small talk with people, but that habit died on the vine. Even if someone had something interesting to say, they wouldn't dare say it. The cameras and monitors everywhere, and the state always watching, have killed off any sense of community, any spark of real human interaction. People have learned to keep their thoughts and feelings buried. Alex watches them now, these people trapped in the digital cage he helped build, and wonders if redemption is even possible.

The automated carpool awaits him outside, lined up behind the other autonomous vehicles, all ready to whisk workers like Alex away to their corporate stations. He steps inside, joining the other passengers who sit in silence, avoiding eye contact. The doors slide shut with a soft hiss, and the vehicle glides through the streets.

He still remembers G.P.S.—hell, he still remembers *maps*—but he doesn't have to give it directions; the system knows where he needs to be, the exact route to take, how long it will take to get there, and how much of his CBDC balance will be deducted for the ride.

Alex stares out the window as the city passes by in a blur of glass and metal punctuated by the occasional drone patrol. Every building looks the same—sleek, featureless, and cold. There's no warmth in the architecture, no uniqueness. Just efficiency.

Even the people he passes on the street are more like extensions of the machines they rely on. Their expressions are blank, their movements mechanical. Everyone is going through the motions of being alive, but no one is actually living.

***

The car pulls up to UmbraCorp, its towering, mirrored façade reflecting the grey sky above. Alex feels the same sinking feeling in his chest that he's felt every day for the past several years. There was a time when he took pride in walking through these doors. Now, it's just another prison—one where he's both guard and inmate.

A device at the entrance scans his wrist as he steps through, logging his arrival in the system. The lobby is immaculate, its polished surfaces gleaming under the bright OLED lights. Workers file in through various checkpoints, silent and focused.

As Alex makes his way to his station, Sarah from Accounting pauses as he passes. There's something tense in her posture that doesn't match her casual tone.

"How's the productivity tracking going?" she asks, adjusting her tablet screen away from any watching eyes.

"Apparently, I achieved 103% efficiency yesterday." Alex grins.

"That's impossible." Sarah's eyes flick to the nearest surveillance camera.

"I know. I reported myself for suspicious overachievement."

Sarah's lips twitch—almost a smile, but not quite. The humor dies in her eyes as she glances around the room before leaning in close. "Chen from Systems Integration didn't show up today," she whispers, her voice barely audible. "They're saying he's being 'adjusted' for questioning the new productivity metrics."

Alex's stomach tightens as he sits down in his cubicle. The screen activates, displaying his daily tasks: monitoring AI feedback loops, ensuring systems function as intended, and correcting minor glitches. Hours of mind-numbing tedium, but that's the point. The system doesn't want creativity or innovation; it wants consistency and predictability.

He types a set of commands into the console, trying to focus on the scrolling code instead of thoughts of Chen. Every keystroke and decision he makes is monitored, logged, and evaluated. His efficiency is scrutinized and factored into his social credit score.

By midday, he's already bone tired. His wrist communicator informs him it's time for his break—not that he has any choice in the matter. The system, as always, keeps track of everything. Even his breaks are automated and timed to ensure maximum productivity, all part of some algorithm he probably helped write.

Alex heads to the corporate café, an expansive, white-walled space filled with neatly arranged tables. There's no warmth here either, no sense of escape from work. The only sounds are the quiet hum of machines preparing food and the murmurs of conversation between other workers, all conducted in hushed tones.

He steps up to the food dispenser, ordering another synthetic meal—this time a nutrient bar and a cup of Caff-ee, a caffeinated liquid that happens to be coffee-flavored. The machine scans his wrist, deducting the cost from his CBDC balance and informing him that his social credit score remains unchanged.

The transactions are as emotionless as the food itself, and Alex wonders, not for the first time, if the system would even notice if he simply stopped coming to work. Would anything really change? He's too afraid to find out. Besides, it's not like he has another better option.

His food arrives with a mechanical beep, and he sits at one of the tables near the window, staring out at the endless stream of drones and autonomous vehicles zipping through the city streets. He takes a sip of the Caff-ee, wincing at the bitter, metallic aftertaste. Just another example of production in a world where enjoyment has been replaced with efficiency.

As Alex eats, his mind drifts. There's something about today that feels heavier than usual, something more pressing than the typical monotony. He watches as the other workers shuffle in and out of the café, their faces expressionless, their movements robotic. It's all just *so*...empty.

A few tables away, an overly cheerful robo-chef delivers a tray of food to one of the workers, chirping out a pre-recorded phrase: *"Have a super productive day!"* Alex can't help but roll his eyes. It's like a toaster telling you to reach for the stars while burning your bread.

The robo-chef glides to his table, its perpetual smile somehow more grating than usual. "Would you like a beverage?" it chirps. "Studies show hydration increases productivity by twelve percent!"

The robot's fake cheerfulness irritates him, and he snaps before he can stop himself. "Just leave me alone. I don't need your productivity statistics."

The moment the words leave his lips, he regrets it. His wrist communicator beeps with an ominous tone. Alex glances down, his stomach sinking as a notification flashes across the screen: *Social Credit Score: -50 points.*

Even the smallest display of discontent, the slightest deviation from the expected behavior, is recorded and punished. Alex knows better than to complain, but today, something inside him snapped—just for a moment—and now he's paying for it.

He clenches his jaw and fights the wave of frustration surging up inside him. It's not just the social credit score; it's everything. The food, the job, and the constant surveillance. His life has been reduced to a series of tasks, transactions, and performance evaluations. There's no room for mistakes, defiance, or anything that isn't part of the system's plan.

He finishes his meal in silence, his thoughts churning with frustration and disillusionment. As he walks back to his cubicle, he can't shake the feeling that something is wrong. Not just with him but with the world.

For years, Alex has tried to ignore it, tried to convince himself that this is just the way things are, that it's easier to go along with the system than to fight it. But today, that denial feels paper-thin. The cracks are starting to show, and for the first time in a long while, Alex wonders if maybe—just maybe—there's another way.

Back at his desk, the rest of the day drags on in the same monotonous routine. He types commands, watches the AI systems respond, corrects minor errors, and repeats the process over and over again. It's mindless work, the kind that doesn't require real thought or creativity—just repetition.

But even as he goes through the motions, his mind continues to wander. His thoughts keep circling back to that moment in the café, to how his social credit score dropped over something so trivial. It's ridiculous, really. He knows it. Everyone knows it. But no one talks about it. No one questions it.

The system is designed to be unquestionable. It's designed to make you doubt yourself, to make you believe that the problem isn't with the world—it's with you.

By the time Alex leaves UmbraCorp for the day, the sky has darkened, the endless twilight giving way to the artificial glow of the city's streetlights. The drones are still there, still watching, still patrolling. Nothing changes in Valhalla Center.

The automated carpool arrives to take him home, and as Alex steps inside, he feels the familiar weight settle on his shoulders. Another day lost to the grind, another day that feels just like the last. The same routine, the same hollow existence. He watches the city rush by through the window, the glow of neon signs and surveillance drones casting harsh reflections against the smooth surfaces of the passing buildings.

Inside the car, there's no conversation, no interaction. Alex leans back in his seat, closing his eyes, but his mind refuses to rest. He can't stop thinking about that notification—the way his social credit score dipped by a fraction of a percent. It was such a small thing, a minor infraction. It's a reminder that the system is always watching, always listening, and always ready to correct anyone who steps out of line, even in the slightest.

His social credit score is more than just a number; it's his access to everything—transportation, food, healthcare. A low score means limited access. Too low, and he could be cut off from the basic necessities of life. And for what? Telling a robot to leave him alone.

As the car glides through the streets, Alex's thoughts drift back to a time before all of this. He can't remember it clearly, but he knows it existed. A time when people didn't have to watch every word they said, when they could speak freely without fear of consequences. A time when human interaction was...real.

But that world feels like a dream fading from memory. He doesn't even know if it ever really existed or if it's just something he's made up—a fantasy to cope with the reality he's trapped in.

The car pulls up to his apartment complex, and Alex steps out, the doors sliding shut behind him. The familiar sound of the city envelops him as he walks toward the building's entrance, the dull thrum of machinery blending with the ever-present hum of drones hovering overhead.

Inside, the apartment is quiet. Mila is still at work and undoubtedly caught up in another late-night project. She's been working more and more lately, disappearing into her job just as Alex has. It's easier that way. Easier to lose yourself in work than to face the emptiness that waits when the day is done.

He collapses onto the couch, letting out a long breath as he stares up at the ceiling. His wrist communicator buzzes again, but he doesn't even bother checking the notification this time. He knows what it is—another reminder, another task, another instruction from the system. It's always something, always demanding his attention and compliance.

The apartment feels too quiet. Alex glances over at the violin hanging on the wall. It's been years since Mila has touched it, and the silence it's left behind feels heavier with each passing day. Music, real music, feels like something from another world now, something that doesn't belong in a place like Valhalla Center. Here, everything is artificial and manufactured, stripped of any real human expression.

Alex gets up and walks to the kitchen. He opens the refrigerator, knowing exactly what he'll find—rows of neatly packaged, synthetic meals. There's no variety, no choice, just the same bland food that's been sustaining them for years. He grabs one of the packages and tears it open, the smell of the nutrient paste filling the air. He doesn't bother with the synthesizer anymore - heating it doesn't make it taste any better.

He sits at the table, staring down at the meal in front of him. It's the same thing he's eaten most nights for as long as he can remember, and yet, each bite feels more and more like an act of resignation. He eats mechanically, not tasting the food, and not caring about the texture. It's just fuel—another necessity in a life that's been stripped of all joy.

As he eats, his mind drifts back to the slip-up at the café. The momentary flicker of frustration that led to a drop in his social credit score. He knows it was a small thing, a tiny infraction in the grand scheme of things, but it feels like more than that. It feels like a crack in the carefully constructed façade he's built around himself.

For so long, Alex has convinced himself that this is just the way things are, that it's easier to go along with the system than to fight it. He's told himself that if he keeps his head down, does his job, and follows the rules, everything will be fine. But lately, that lie has become harder to maintain and the truth harder to ignore. People aren't meant to live like this—trapped in fear, settling for survival instead of really living.

The truth is, he isn't depressed—he's absolutely miserable. He's trapped in a system that values numbers and productivity over humanity, a system that watches and controls every aspect of his life. And he's tired of pretending that it isn't eating away at him, slowly but surely.

The sense of emptiness again settles over him. He pushes the tray away, the half-eaten food staring back at him, a reminder of the life he's resigned himself to. He can't do this anymore. He can't keep living like this, going through the motions of a life that no longer feels like his own.

But what choice does he have? The system doesn't just punish disobedience—it monitors everything from facial expressions to heart rates, social media activity to spending patterns, flagging anyone who shows signs of dissatisfaction. There's no escaping it, no fighting it. Even if he wanted to, even if he could muster the courage to rebel, what difference would it make? He's just one man, one insignificant cog in a machine that spans the entire world.

And then there are the fates of those who try to fight back. Brain re-programming, years in labor camps, solitary confinement in private buildings that are functional prisons. He's heard rumblings of even worse fates. And these fates, to his mind, are worse than death.

Alex stands up from the table, the chair scraping against the floor as he pushes it back. He walks to the window, staring out at the city beyond. Neon lights flicker in the distance, casting an eerie glow over the towering skyscrapers. The drones continue their endless patrols, red eyes scanning the streets below for any sign of dissent.

He watches them for a long time, his mind racing with thoughts he doesn't want to confront. Thoughts about the system, his place in it, the life he's living—or not living. He tells himself that it's easier this way, as he has so many times before. It's easier to just go along with it, do his job, and follow the rules. It's easier to deny the truth than to face it.

But as he stands there, staring out at the cold, lifeless city, the discomfort grows inside him. It's the realization that he's been lying to himself for years. He's been telling himself that this is all there is, that this is the best humanity can do. But deep down, he knows it's not true.

Deep down, he knows there's more to life than this. He just doesn't know where to find it or how to obtain it; they've taken away any avenues toward doing so.

He turns away from the window, his chest tight with frustration and fear. He's not ready to admit it, not entirely. There's a nagging voice in the back of his mind telling him that something is wrong, that something needs to change.

For now, all he can do is bury it. He tells himself that it's just another day, that tomorrow will be better, that the system isn't as bad as it seems.

He could have it worse—that's what he tells himself. But he knows that's what everyone under a regime like this tells themselves.

As Alex heads to bed, the lights dim automatically, and he slips under the covers. He knows the truth is there, just beneath the surface, winking at him and baiting him. He'll have the courage to engage it one day. But today isn't the day. He falls into a deep sleep, his only amnesty from this soul-sapping existence.

Chapter 3

Lux Veritatis

A lex steps out of UmbraCorp as the cold, artificial wind whips through the streets. The sky is the same dull grey, and the lights from the buildings cast long shadows over the pavement. His eyes sting from hours of staring at screens, but the numbness in his soul is worse. It's always worse at the end of the day—when he has nothing but the deadening routine behind him and nothing ahead but another night of synthetic food and silence. Even surrounded by his family, he feels alone—Mila is lost in her work projects, Jackson is deep in his virtual world, and neither is questioning the system that is slowly killing their humanity. Sometimes, he thinks that having them there but unreachable is worse than if he were alone.

The doors slide shut behind him, and he breathes in the stale, metallic-tinted air of the city. There's something deeply wrong with the way it tastes. It's not the pollution—it's the fact that he can't even remember what fresh air used to taste like. The gnawing emptiness in his chest is a constant reminder that his life has been reduced to a series of tasks dictated by an unfeeling machine.

He stuffs his hands into his coat pockets and begins the familiar walk home. The automated carpool is there, as always, waiting to take him wherever the system says he needs to go. But today, for reasons he can't quite put into words, Alex doesn't get in. He doesn't feel like riding in a silent, controlled space today. He wants to walk and feel the ground under his feet.

No one walks here unless they have to. Everyone is either inside a vehicle or behind glass, their lives dictated by the flow of CBDC transactions and social credit scores. Pedestrians have become relics of a forgotten time, like the trees that once lined these streets.

Alex's steps echo on the concrete, and he feels the weight of the day settle deeper into his bones. He walks without a destination, his thoughts swirling in the same monotonous patterns they always do. Work. Home. Repeat. There's no room for anything else in this city, in this life. And yet, beneath the surface, something stirs—a whisper of discontent he's been trying to ignore for months.

As he rounds a corner, something catches his eye. At first, it seems unremarkable—just a figure standing near a streetlamp, head down, face hidden by the collar of a long coat. The stranger is still, too still, as if waiting for something. Or someone. Alex slows his pace, his hand brushing against his wrist communicator. He doesn't know why, but something about the figure unsettles him.

The stranger looks up just as Alex passes, their eyes meeting for a brief moment. The man's face is ordinary, forgettable even, but there's something in his expression—a knowing look, a subtle challenge—that makes Alex hesitate. The stranger doesn't speak at first; he just watches Alex with an intensity that feels out of place in a city where everyone avoids eye contact.

"Late night?" the man asks, his voice casual but with a hint of something more. Given the time, it's a strange question—only a little after the workday has ended. But there's a weight to it, as if he's asking something else entirely.

Alex pauses, unsure how to respond. He glances around, expecting to see one of the ever-present drones hovering nearby, but the street is empty. Unusually so.

The man smiles—a small, knowing smile that doesn't reach his eyes. "You don't get out much, do you?"

Alex frowns, the discomfort in his chest growing. "I get out when I need to," he replies more defensively than necessary.

"Ah, need," the man says with a nod as if that single word explains everything. He steps closer, but his movements appear unthreatening. "Funny thing, need. It's all about control, isn't it? The system tells us what we need and when we need it. What to eat, where to go, what to say." He pauses, his eyes flicking to Alex's wrist communicator. "Even when to breathe, if we let it."

Alex's mouth goes dry. There's something off about this conversation. Something dangerous. He should leave, keep walking, and get back into the carpool. But his feet don't move.

The stranger seems to sense his hesitation. "Relax," he says, his voice dropping to a lower tone. "I'm not with *them*. But I know what you're thinking." He reaches into his coat and pulls out a small, folded pamphlet, holding it out to Alex. "You should read this. It's...enlightening."

Alex stares at the pamphlet for a moment, not reaching for it. He glances up at the stranger, suspicion prickling the back of his neck. "What is it?"

"Nothing that'll get you in trouble," the man says with a smirk. "Unless, of course, you think too hard about it. Then it might change your life. But don't worry—no one will know. The system's blind to things like this."

Alex's hand moves on its own, reaching out and taking the pamphlet before he can stop himself. The paper is thin, crinkled at the edges, and oddly tangible in a world where information is delivered through screens. It feels...real.

The stranger's eyes flick up to the nearest streetlight, where a small, blinking red light indicates the presence of a surveillance camera. "It's best appreciated in solitude," he whispers. "Maybe over a cup of Cryptobucks coffee. Somewhere quiet, where you can think without being watched."

Alex tucks the pamphlet into his coat pocket, his mind racing. The man's words are cryptic, filled with irony and sarcasm, but Alex understands the message. He knows exactly what the stranger is implying: the system can't monitor everything. There are cracks in the façade and blind spots in the all-seeing eye of the GSF. But why him? Why now?

Before he can ask another question, the stranger steps back into the shadows, disappearing into the haze of the city. Alex stands there for a long time, unsure of what just happened. His heart pounds in his chest, fear and curiosity swirling in his gut. He knows he should throw the pamphlet away and pretend this encounter never happened. But his hand tightens around it instead, his fingers crimping the edges as he starts walking again.

By the time Alex reaches a small, dingy café on the corner of 5th and Hanover, the sky has darkened and the city's neon lights cast an unnatural glow over everything. He slips inside, grateful for the dim lighting and the lack of customers. It's not a place frequented by the city's usual corporate drones—too rundown, too analog. It's the perfect spot to read something dangerous without prying eyes.

He orders a cup of Cryptobucks coffee from the worn-out machine in the corner, the robotic arm delivering it with a cheery "Enjoy your day!" that feels more like a threat than a courtesy. Alex slides into a booth in the back, where the seat is sticky from years of neglect, and pulls the pamphlet from his pocket.

The title on the front seems harmless enough: *A Better Tomorrow?*

Alex opens it, reading the text. It starts out like any other piece of propaganda—polished, reassuring, filled with hollow promises of progress and unity. But as he reads further, the tone shifts, becoming sharp, biting. Sarcasm and irony drip from the words, each sentence layered with subtext that the GSF's AI systems wouldn't catch.

"Isn't it great that we live in such a perfect society?" the pamphlet reads. *A society where no one goes hungry because we all eat the same tasteless sludge, and no one feels alone because we're always being watched. It's so wonderful that we don't have to worry about privacy anymore because who needs privacy when you have security?*

Alex can't help but smirk. The message is clear: this isn't a celebration of the system. It's a condemnation—a warning wrapped in irony. And the more he reads, the more uncomfortable he becomes.

The pamphlet talks about how the GSF controls everything—not just the economy or the food supply, but how people think through a web of control: mandatory state broadcasts that repeat the same messages day after day, AI-curated entertainment that subtly rewards compliance, social credit bonuses for sharing approved opinions, automated 'wellness-checks' that flag any deviation from standard behavior patterns. It shows how they shape people's actions and sense of self through constant surveillance and manipulation.

It describes how the CBDC and social credit systems are tools of oppression designed to manipulate behavior and stifle dissent. It tells stories of other societies—historical examples of authoritarian regimes that controlled their populations in eerily similar ways. And with each example, the pamphlet asks the same sarcastic question: *Isn't it great that we don't live like that?*

But Alex knows the truth. This is exactly how they live. The pamphlet is describing his life and his world. The GSF has a hand in everything, shaping every aspect of society down to the most personal details. And yet, most people, Alex included, have accepted it as normal and unavoidable. As he reads on, a cold realization begins to settle over him: he's been complicit in this system for years. He's been playing his role, staying quiet, and keeping his head down while the walls of his prison were being built higher and higher until there was no longer any way out.

The pamphlet goes on, each sentence like a needle pricking at the fragile bubble of denial Alex has wrapped himself in for so long.

And isn't it just wonderful that we're all so free? Free to work the same jobs every day, free to eat the same tasteless food, and free to be "productive" citizens under the watchful gaze of the drones. Who needs a choice when you have the illusion of it?

Alex clenches his fist, crumpling the corner of the pamphlet. He's not sure if it's anger or fear that makes his chest tighten, but something cracks inside him, something he's been holding back for far too long.

The pamphlet doesn't stop there. It talks about the GSF's surveillance programs and how every word and every action is monitored and categorized. But, the pamphlet points out with dripping sarcasm, *isn't it comforting to know that someone is always watching over us? After all, if you have nothing to hide, you have nothing to fear.*

That line hits Alex hard. He's heard it so many times before—on the propaganda channels, from his colleagues, even from Mila when they've argued about the GSF's policies. It's the lie they've all been told, the lie they've all accepted. But the truth is there, staring back at him from the worn pages of the pamphlet.

Everyone has something to hide, even if it's just the simple, unspoken desire to be left alone.

As he reads, the words begin to blur. His mind is racing, thoughts colliding and spiraling out of control. Everything he's believed, or pretended to believe, is unraveling. The GSF doesn't protect them. It controls them. The CBDC isn't just currency; it's a leash. The social credit system isn't about rewarding good behavior but punishing those who dare to step out of line.

The pamphlet ends with a statement, one that sends a shiver down Alex's spine: *We've been waiting for you.*

For a long time, Alex just stares at the page, the words echoing in his mind. Waiting for him? For what? He doesn't want to think about it. He doesn't want to admit what the pamphlet is really asking of him.

It's calling on him to resist.

The realization is a cold, hard knot in his stomach. This isn't just some piece of dangerous literature. This is a call to action, a signal from the resistance movement he's only heard whispers about—Voxx Pop. They're real. And they're watching. The pamphlet was handed to him for a reason.

His hands tremble slightly as he folds the pamphlet back up and stuffs it into his pocket. The café feels too small now, too exposed. He glances around, suddenly hyperaware of every little noise and every flicker of movement. The surveillance cameras on the street outside might not be able to detect the irony and sarcasm in the pamphlet's words, but the GSF's reach is long. If they knew what he was thinking right now, what he had just read, they'd find a way to silence him. That's what they do to dissenters.

But what terrifies Alex even more is the growing sense that the GSF doesn't have to silence him. They don't need to. They've already won, in a way. They've made sure that no one *wants* to resist. They've made the world outside the system feel so dangerous and so impossible that even the thought of stepping out of line feels like madness.

He presses a hand to his forehead, trying to steady his breathing. What is he supposed to do with this? He's just one man. One man in a city engineered to crush dissent and break anyone who tries to stand up to the machine. How could he possibly make a difference? How could anyone?

We've been waiting for you.

Alex gathers his things, feeling a strange urgency to leave the café, but a flicker of doubt creeps back in as he stands. He's been comfortable in his denial for so long, and now the reality is too overwhelming. What would Mila think if she knew he was reading something like this? She believes in the system. She's convinced that the GSF, with all its flaws, keeps them safe from the chaos outside. She'd never forgive him for even entertaining these thoughts.

Jackson, too. Alex spent so long telling his son to follow the rules, to not rock the boat, and now here he was, considering whether to do the very thing he's warned Jackson against: questioning the system.

The door to the café opens with a chime, and Alex's heart skips a beat. But it's just another customer, their eyes fixed on the floor, moving with the same mechanical detachment as everyone else. He breathes out a sigh of relief, but the anxiety doesn't fade.

He stands frozen, staring at the door. He knows he should leave. He should go home, bury the pamphlet somewhere, and forget this ever happened. It's safer that way. Easier. But he can't shake the feeling that something's shifted inside him, that even if he throws the pamphlet away, the questions it's raised will remain.

As he steps outside, the night air feels colder than usual, and the weight of the city seems to press down on him from all sides. The surveillance drones continue their silent patrols, and the streetlights cast long, unnatural shadows on the pavement. He tucks his hands into his pockets, his fingers brushing against the crumpled pamphlet. He knows he can't just ignore it now. The words are etched into his mind, and they won't leave him alone.

Alex walks home slowly, his thoughts a chaotic mess of fear, anger, and uncertainty. The GSF's grip on the city is absolute, and yet there are cracks in the system—cracks that people like the stranger he met are trying to exploit. Voxx Pop. The resistance. The idea seems both ridiculous and terrifying at the same time. How could they possibly succeed? The GSF controls everything—every aspect of life. How could anyone believe they have a chance against such overwhelming power?

And yet, part of him is tempted. The system has taken everything from him. He's spent years going through the motions, convincing himself that it's easier to just follow the rules and keep his head down. But the truth is, he's been dying inside, piece by piece.

By the time Alex reaches his apartment, the sky is completely dark, and the neon lights from the buildings cast an eerie glow over the city. He hesitates at the door, hand hovering over the sensor. Inside is the life he knows—his prison. But outside...outside is the unknown.

He presses the sensor that triggers the retinal scan, and the door slides open. The apartment is quiet and dimly lit. Mila is still at work, and Jackson is probably lost in his VR world again. The loneliness feels heavier than ever, pressing down on him like a weight he can't shake.

As he steps inside, Alex pulls the pamphlet from his pocket and holds it up to the light, reading the final line again: *We've been waiting for you.*

He folds it carefully and tucks it into a drawer, hidden away for now. But he knows he can't hide from it forever. The questions, the doubt, and the growing discomfort with the world he lives in—it's all there, simmering beneath the surface, waiting for the moment when he can no longer pretend it doesn't exist.

He stands in the middle of the room, staring at the drawer where he's hidden the pamphlet, torn between the only life he knows and the idea that these people think Alex could help liberate the masses.

Could he, Alex Vanguard, make a real, noticeable difference? He doesn't know for certain, but he turns off that thought train before he turns off the light.

Chapter 4

Alpha-Omega

The following day, Alex wakes before dawn, the dim light of the city's perpetual haze filtering through the thin blinds. For a few moments, he lies there in the stillness, listening to the air filtration system and Mila's breathing as she sleeps. His mind feels heavy, as though weighed down by something he can't quite place, but it doesn't take long for the events of the previous night to flood back in.

The pamphlet. Voxx Pop. The stranger's knowing gaze. The words *"We've been waiting for you"* still echo in his mind, a challenge and a warning wrapped in subversive irony.

For a brief moment, Alex considers getting out of bed, going to the drawer where he stashed the pamphlet, and tossing it in the garbage chute. It would be so easy to forget about all of it—to pretend the encounter never happened and bury the questions and doubts before they take root.

But even as the thought crosses his mind, he knows it's too late for that. Something inside him has already shifted. The cracks in his carefully constructed facade are growing, and the truths the pamphlet revealed—truths he's tried to ignore for so long—are becoming harder to deny.

Still, he hesitates. The idea of investigating Voxx Pop, of learning more about the resistance, terrifies him. What if the GSF finds out? What if they come for him, for Mila, for Jackson? The fear grips his chest like a vice, and he forces himself to push it away.

"I can't do this," he mutters under his breath. He sits up, swinging his legs over the side of the bed. His wrist communicator buzzes, the morning newsfeed flashing across the screen. *President Kleton Announces New AI Reforms to Strengthen Public Safety* reads one of the headlines. Alex scoffs. *Public safety*—yet another euphemism for surveillance, control, and the tightening grip of the GSF.

He can't help but glance toward the drawer, where the pamphlet still lies hidden, its message waiting like a spark ready to ignite. He should destroy it. That's what a rational man would do. But he's not feeling rational today. For once, Alex feels something stirring inside him—curiosity, anger, or maybe just frustration. He can't quite tell. All he knows is that the hollow feeling that's been growing inside him is reaching a point where ignoring it is no longer possible.

The AI assistant chimes softly from his communicator. *Time to prepare for work, Alex.*

His routine waits for him, the same monotonous grind at UmbraCorp, the same lifeless tasks that have defined his days for years. He goes through the motions of getting ready—showering, dressing, grabbing a nutrient bar from the kitchen—but all the while, his mind is elsewhere. The pamphlet's words, the sarcasm and irony, the way it mocked the very system Alex is a part of...It all feels too real now.

The carpool arrives at the usual time, and as Alex steps inside, he finds himself wondering if the stranger is still out there somewhere, waiting for him to act. Waiting for him to make a choice.

The morning passes in a blur of meaningless tasks. Alex's hands move mechanically over the console, inputting data, monitoring AI feedback loops, and correcting minor system glitches. But his mind is a thousand miles away. He can't focus on the work. Can't shake the feeling that something is about to change.

Around midday, he steps away from his station, heading for the corporate café where he orders the same flavorless synthetic meal as always. He sits at one of the sterile tables, staring out the window as the drones patrol the streets below. The city moves in its carefully controlled rhythms, each person playing their part, each system functioning exactly as designed.

Alex feels the weight of it all pressing down on him—the endless surveillance, the suffocating control, the way algorithms and AI dictate every aspect of life. He should feel comforted by the order and safety the GSF promises. But all he feels is trapped.

He reaches into his pocket, half-expecting to find the pamphlet there, even though he knows it's still in the drawer at home. The questions it raised are still gnawing at him, refusing to be silenced. What if Voxx Pop is right? What if everything he's believed is a lie?

His mind flashes to Mila. She's always been the practical one, the one who believes in the system's necessity, even if she doesn't always agree with its methods. She used to argue with Alex whenever he voiced even the slightest dissatisfaction with the way things were. *"It's the best system we have,"* she'd say. *"It keeps us safe. It keeps us alive."*

But does it? Alex wonders. *Does it really?*

The thought unsettles him, and he pushes it away, burying it beneath the routine of the day. He finishes his meal quickly, the taste lingering like ash in his mouth, and returns to his station, trying to lose himself in the work.

But the questions don't go away.

The sky is already dark when Alex leaves work that evening. The streets are quiet, the weight of the day settling into his bones as he walks toward the carpool. His mind still churns with doubt and uncertainty. The tension that's been building inside him is reaching a breaking point, and he can't ignore it for much longer.

When he arrives home, Mila is still at work, and Jackson is in his room. Alex feels a pang of guilt, a familiar ache that comes from knowing how distant he's become from his son.

He heads into the kitchen and opens the cupboard to grab another synthetic meal. As he eats, his wrist communicator buzzes with a notification. It's from Jackson's school—a formal message from the state education board.

Alex taps the screen, his stomach tightening.

Congratulations, Mr. Vanguard! Your son, Jackson Vanguard, has been selected for a state-sponsored scholarship as part of the Elite Academic Initiative. Jackson's

performance in the fields of virtual design and AI programming has been exem-
plary, and we are pleased to offer him the opportunity to attend the prestigious
Valhalla Center Institute of Technological Excellence. This scholarship is reserved
for only the top 0.01% of students in the nation, and we are confident that Jackson's
talents will continue to develop under the guidance of the Institute's esteemed faculty-

.

Alex stares at the message while his heart sinks. The scholarship should be a cause for celebration—a sign that Jackson's future is secure. But all Alex feels is dread. He knows what the scholarship means. It's not just an opportunity for Jackson to advance; it's the state sinking its claws even deeper into his son, drawing him further into the machine.

He sets the meal aside, his appetite gone. His hands shake as he taps the communicator, pulling up Jackson's academic profile. Everything looks perfect, just as the message said—top scores in every subject, a glowing recommendation from his teachers, and praise for his innovative use of AI in virtual environments. It's everything a parent should want for their child.

But Alex can't shake the feeling that something is terribly wrong. The GSF has been watching Jackson for years, monitoring his progress, shaping him into the perfect citizen. And with this scholarship, they'll have even more control over his future. Jackson is already so immersed in the virtual world and so disconnected from reality and his family. What will happen to him once he's fully under the state's influence?

Alex runs a hand through his hair. He could refuse the scholarship. He could tell Jackson that it's not the right path for him and that there are other ways to succeed. But would Jackson even listen? Would Mila agree?

He stands up from the table and paces the room. His thoughts are spinning, the tension building inside him like a coiled spring. The pamphlet, the stranger, the resistance—all of it feels distant now, overshadowed by the immediate reality of what's happening to his son.

But the two are connected, aren't they? The GSF, the control, the scholar-ship—it's all part of the same system, the same machine that's been grinding him down for years. The same machine that's now pulling Jackson deeper into its grasp.

Alex's eyes flick to Jackson's door, where the soft glow of the VR headset still flickers. His son is lost in a virtual paradise, unaware of the forces shaping his future and the decision his father is now grappling with.

Is it worth it? Alex wonders. Is it worth pursuing the truth and uncovering the depths of the GSF's control if it means putting his family at risk? What if Voxx Pop is wrong? What if the resistance fails, and the GSF discovers his involvement? What will happen to Mila? To Jackson?

The fear gnaws at him. It's a constant, insistent whisper in the back of his mind. He's just one man. How could he possibly stand against the GSF? And even if he wanted to, how could he risk everything—his job, his life, his family—for a cause that might be hopeless? Would fighting back make up for what he helped create, or would it just endanger his family?

Alex moves to the living room, collapsing onto the couch as the weight of it all presses down on him. He stares at the ceiling, trying to calm the storm of thoughts swirling in his mind, but nothing helps. The tension won't leave. The questions won't stop. Neither will the responsibility for what he's done.

He thinks of Jackson, the little boy who spent hours building towers out of blocks, imagining grand cities and worlds beyond this one. He thinks of how proud he was when Jackson first started experimenting with virtual design and how his son's mind seemed to soar, filled with creativity and promise. But now, that creativity is being channeled into something darker, something controlled by the state. The scholarship is proof of that. The GSF has noticed Jackson's talents, and now they're pulling him further into the system, molding him into exactly what they want.

The realization dawns. Jackson isn't just another student. He's becoming part of the machine—part of the very system that Alex has come to hate. And soon, if Alex doesn't do something, Jackson will be too far gone, lost to the state forever.

Alex stands abruptly, his hands clenched into fists. His breath comes fast, his heart pounding in his chest. He's never felt this kind of urgency before, this kind of terror. The thought of Jackson being swallowed by the GSF and turned into another cog in the machine—it's unbearable.

But what can he do? The question echoes in his mind, taunting him. He could speak to Jackson and try to explain what's really happening. But Jackson, like so many others, has already been indoctrinated by the state's propaganda. He believes in the system and trusts it. He's grown up in a world where dissent is seen as madness, where questioning authority is dangerous. What could Alex say that wouldn't sound like the ramblings of a paranoid conspiracy theorist?

And then there's Mila. She's always been pragmatic and focused on survival. She's never wanted to rock the boat. She believes that the GSF, for all its faults, keeps them safe. How could Alex tell her that he's considering throwing all of that away and thinking about defying the system they've both worked so hard to survive within? How could he explain that he's been drawn into something dangerous that could destroy everything they've built?

The pressure is too much. Alex rakes a hand over his face and feels like he's being torn between his duty to his family and the growing need to confront the truth. *Isn't it great that we don't live like this?* The pamphlet's words flash in his mind again, mocking him. The reality is, they do live like this. And the more Alex thinks about it, the more he realizes that he's been lying to himself for far too long.

He walks to the bedroom, his gaze settling on the drawer where he hid the pamphlet. His fingers hover over the handle for a moment, trembling slightly, before he pulls it open. The crinkled pamphlet lies there, just as he left it, a small but undeniable reminder of the choice he now faces.

He unfolds it slowly, reading the words again and letting them sink in. The sarcasm, the irony—they're tools, weapons against the system's blindness. The AI can't understand the layers of hidden meaning in the text. But Alex can. And as he reads, something stirs inside him—a spark of defiance, a flicker of resistance.

But is it enough?

His thoughts return to Jackson, the scholarship, and the path his son is now on. If Alex does nothing, Jackson will become just another pawn in the state's game, another mind controlled by the GSF. But if Alex acts—if he embraces the resistance and joins Voxx Pop—what will that mean for his family? What will happen to Mila and Jackson if the GSF finds out?

The risks are enormous. The consequences are unthinkable. He's seen what happens to those who resist—the labor camps, the brain reprogramming, entire families separated and never heard from again. And those are just the fates they let people know about.

Alex folds the pamphlet again, his hands shaking. He knows the choice he's facing. Stay silent, stay safe, and let the GSF continue its control over his family. Or take a stand, join the resistance, and risk everything.

For a long time, he stands there staring at the folded pamphlet in his hand while the weight of the decision presses down on him.

Then, with a heavy sigh, he tucks the pamphlet back into the drawer and closes it. The stakes are too high. He can't afford to act recklessly, not when Jackson's future hangs in the balance.

But the questions remain. The doubt, the unease—they're still there, simmering beneath the surface, waiting for the moment when Alex can no longer ignore them.

As he heads to bed that night, the weight of the day is still heavy on his shoulders. He knows one thing for sure: the time for pretending is over. The only question is whether the time for action is now.

That's a question that can wait until morning, though, he tells himself. And then he reminds himself that he can keep waiting until morning...until one day, he'll wake up and be seventy-five, with no memory of a life worth living and no hope for a new one. Deep down, he already knows he can't keep playing this waiting game—each morning of inaction is another small surrender to the system he claims to hate.

Chapter 5

Cog vs. Cognition

The apartment is dark, save for the blue glow coming from Jackson's room. Alex stands in the hallway, staring at the crack under the door where the blue light flickers occasionally. It's the telltale sign that Jackson is once again lost in the virtual world, absorbed in some distant, simulated paradise.

Alex clenches his fists, feeling the cold fear and frustration settle deeper in his chest. This is becoming more than just a habit for Jackson; it's an addiction, an escape that is getting harder and harder to break. And the worst part? Alex understands all too well why Jackson prefers the artificial world over the empty, hollow one beyond their apartment walls.

But that doesn't make it any easier to bear.

He knocks once, the sound echoing louder than expected in the otherwise silent apartment. "Jackson? You got a minute, bud?"

No response. Just the light seeping out under the door.

Alex's patience is wearing thin. He knocks again, harder this time. "Jackson!"

Still nothing.

With a grimace, Alex turns the handle and pushes the door open. Blue light floods the hallway as he steps inside, the holographic boundary of the VR system bathing Jackson's still figure in its glow. His son lies sprawled on his bed, his body motionless and his mind completely detached from the real world.

Alex takes a deep breath, steps across the room, and yanks the headset off with a firm tug.

Jackson flinches and sits bolt upright, blinking against the sudden intrusion of reality. "Dad! Come *on!*" His voice is angry and offended, as if Alex has just stolen something precious from him. "I was in the middle of something!"

"I know," Alex replies. "And that's the problem."

Jackson rubs his eyes, blinking as he adjusts to the bright light. "You can't just come in here and rip me out like that."

"Look, I'm...I'm sorry, but we gotta talk."

Jackson slumps back onto the bed, still clearly irritated, then spreads his arms. "About what? What's so goddamn important?"

"Language. And...well, this," Alex says, gesturing around the room, his voice growing more intense with every word. "About how you're always plugged in, lost in that...thing. You're never *here*. You're like a...vessel. A body without a soul. A mind detached from its body. I don't know. Do you even realize how much time you spend in there?"

Jackson rolls his eyes. "Oh, seriously? This again? I don't get what the big issue is! It's better in there than out here. I actually enjoy myself in VR. Tell me that I'm missing something great in *this* reality. Come on, tell me."

That strikes a nerve. Alex feels his chest tighten, his jaw clenching. He knows Jackson is right—life in Valhalla Center is a far cry from great and a country mile from what anyone would call fulfilling. But that doesn't make it okay. It's not real.

"That's the problem," Alex snaps as his frustration spills over. "At least it is reality. That VR world's not real, Jackson. You're interacting with people who might not even exist."

Jackson frowns, sitting up straighter. "What are you going on about? Of course they exist. I'm talking to real people. Trust me, I know the difference."

"Do you?" Alex presses, his voice edged with concern.

Jackson raises an eyebrow. "Of course."

Alex steps closer, folding his arms across his chest as he searches for the right words to explain. "Most of what we think is the internet—most of what we interact with, especially in VR—isn't real. It's just sims, bots, algos. You might think you're talking to real people, but you're not. You're just talking to programs designed to trick you."

"Trick me into what?"

"Into thinking you're less alone," Alex says with a gulp.

Jackson scoffs, shaking his head. "Okay, no offense, but you're talking crazy. I know when I'm talking to a real person, Dad. That is just some paranoid conspiracy nonsense."

"Is it?" Alex counters. "How do you know? The GSF controls everything. How do you know they're not using AI to manipulate what you see and what you feel? Do you really know what's real anymore?"

Jackson's face hardens. "I know the difference. I've made friends in VR. We talk, and we hang out. They're real people, not bots."

Alex softens his tone, sensing that the argument is only pushing Jackson further away. "That's the point, Jackson. The system has gotten so good at creating fake interactions that you wouldn't be able to tell. Hell, *I* wouldn't be able to tell. That's the whole idea—they're designed to feel real to make you believe you're part of something genuine."

Jackson shakes his head, his voice tired and frustrated. "Dad, to use a phrase from your generation: you're tripping. You always do this. VR is just...better. It's fun. It's not some massive conspiracy to trick me. Like, I'm sorry you hate your life, but..."

"I don't hate my life," Alex lies unconvincingly.

"Right. Okay. Just...can't I do what makes me happy? I complete my schoolwork with good grades. What else do you want?"

Alex stares at him for a long moment, his heart heavy. He knows Jackson truly believes what he's saying. But he can't shake the nagging feeling that his son is being pulled deeper into something dangerous, something designed to control him, just like everything else in Valhalla Center.

"It's not just VR I'm worried about," Alex says quietly as he sits down on the bed next to Jackson. "It's everything. You're getting more and more disconnected from reality. And now, with this scholarship..."

Jackson's eyes go wide. "Wait, what about the scholarship?"

Alex sighs, running a hand through his hair. "It's not just a reward for your talent, Jackson. The GSF picks the best people to...mold, to pull you deeper into their system. The more you're tied to them, the more control they'll have over you. Don't you want to become yourself?"

Jackson's expression shifts to anger, his jaw tightening. "I am myself, and I'll always *be* myself! You're being paranoid. I earned that scholarship. It's not some conspiracy. You're just...what, are you jealous or something? That I might get to do something cool with my life?"

Alex recoils slightly, feeling the sting of Jackson's words. He isn't jealous. He's scared. Scared of losing his son to a system that has already taken so much from him. But how can he explain that? How can he make Jackson see what's really at stake?

"I'm not jealous, buddy," Alex says softly, struggling to keep his voice steady. "I want the best for you. Always. I just don't want to lose you."

Jackson looks away, his anger simmering but fading. "You're not losing me, Dad. I'm still here. I'm just...I'm just trying to figure things out."

Alex takes a deep breath, searching for a way to break through to his son. And then he remembers the pamphlet. The encrypted message. The cryptic words that have been weighing on him since the moment the stranger handed it to him.

100%

"Speaking of figuring things out..." Alex reaches into his pocket and pulls out the crumpled pamphlet. He hands it to Jackson. "I need your help with something."

Jackson sits up next to him and frowns as he unfolds the pamphlet, his irritation replaced by curiosity. His eyes scan the text, and after a few moments, his expression shifts from confusion to fascination.

"What the hell?" Jackson asks, flipping the paper over. "This looks...well, old. *Really* old."

"It is," Alex says, watching his son closely. "But there's something more to it. There's a QR code, but I don't know how to scan it without being detected."

Jackson's frown deepens as he runs his fingers over the edges of the pamphlet. Then, after a few seconds, his eyes light up with recognition.

"Oh, I know what this is. This is ancient tech," Jackson mutters, his eyes darting around the room as if the walls hold the answer. "I've seen something like this before."

Alex leans in, his heart racing. "What do you mean?"

Jackson looks up, a slight smile on his face. "It's old-school blockchain encryption. Way before the GSF took control of everything. It can only be accessed with ancient tech."

"Ancient tech?" Alex repeats, frowning. "What kind of tech?"

Jackson stands up and heads to his closet, rummaging through a box filled with old gadgets. After a few moments, he pulls out a smartphone, its screen scratched from years of use. "This should do it."

Alex stares at the device, feeling a strange mix of disbelief and gratitude. "Wow. You've had a smartphone all this time?"

"Yeah," Jackson shrugs, powering up the old phone. "I mean, it still works. Barely. But it runs on tech the GSF can't track. If there's an encrypted message in there, this should decrypt it."

Alex watches as Jackson scans the pamphlet using the phone's camera. The screen flickers, lines of code appearing briefly before the decryption process finishes.

"There," Jackson says, handing the phone back to Alex. "It's decrypted, but I don't know what the message says. Because *I* respect others' privacy."

Jackson smirks at his dad, and Alex shakes his head, both impressed by his son's ingenuity and sad that it'll go to waste helping the state.

Alex takes the phone, feeling its weight in his hand. "Thanks, buddy," he says quietly.

Jackson looks at him for a moment, his expression softening. "Just...be careful, okay? I don't know what this is, but it feels...sketchy."

"I know," Alex says softly, his voice steady but tinged with the same uncertainty that grips him. Alt-tests are used to keep citizens in line; if you fail one, you can get a massive deduction—or worse. "I'll be careful. I promise."

Jackson nods, still unconvinced, but he lets it go. "Night, Dad," he mutters, and Alex retreats from the room with the ancient smartphone in his hands and the decrypted message waiting to be revealed.

***

Later that night, when the apartment has fallen silent and Jackson has disappeared back into his virtual world, Alex steps out onto the small balcony. The air is cooler than usual, a sharp contrast to the staleness inside. It feels good against his skin, refreshing even as he stands there staring out at the city beyond. Valhalla Center glows with its artificial light, a sterile maze of towering structures, all controlled, all under the watchful eyes of the GSF.

For years, Alex had learned to ignore it—the way the system wrapped around the city like a noose, tightening with every passing day. But tonight, standing here with the smartphone in his hand and the weight of the unknown pressing against him, it's impossible to ignore.

He pulls out the phone, the glow of the screen dim against the backdrop of the city lights. His heart pounds as he taps the screen to unlock it and brings up the decoded message. His hand tightens around the device as he reads the single word.

Welcome...

Alex stares at the word for what feels like an eternity. It's just one word, but it's charged with so much meaning. It pulses on the screen, almost as if it's alive—inviting him into something deeper, something far beyond the pamphlet and the cryptic words it contained.

This isn't just a message. It's an invitation. The realization hits him with the weight of finality—he's being pulled into something much bigger than he ever imagined. Voxx Pop, the resistance, the stranger who had handed him the pamphlet—this was just the beginning.

Alex's mind races with questions, fear gnawing at the edges of his thoughts. *Welcome to what?* The word seems to mock him, daring him to step further into a world that promises danger and truth in equal measure.

For years, he's lived with the slow, suffocating feeling that everything in Valhalla Center is wrong. That the GSF, with all its control, has stripped away any sense of freedom, any spark of real life. And now, standing on the precipice of something real, something that could change everything, Alex feels the weight of that choice pressing down on him.

He takes a deep breath, leaning against the railing, the cold metal pressing into his palm. The city stretches out before him, vast and unyielding, and yet in this moment, it feels smaller somehow. The GSF has missed something. They haven't seen this. They haven't seen him.

Welcome...

The word keeps pulsing on the screen, and Alex knows he's being invited into something far more dangerous than just encrypted messages and ironic pamphlets. This is a call to action, an invitation into a world that exists outside the GSF's iron grip. But it's also a warning.

He knows there's no going back now. The door has been opened, and whatever waits on the other side will change everything—his life, his family's future, and the fragile existence they've built in this controlled city.

A sharp sense of dread courses through him as he stands on the balcony, staring at the word. He thinks of Jackson back in his room, immersed in the virtual world that offers so much comfort and escape. He thinks of Mila, still at work and still believing that the GSF, for all its faults, keeps them safe. And then he thinks of the stranger who handed him the pamphlet that said, *We've been waiting for you.*

Had Voxx Pop been watching him this whole time? Had they seen something in him that even he hadn't recognized? A willingness to fight back, to resist?

Alex swallows hard, his throat dry. He didn't sign up for this. He didn't plan on becoming part of a resistance movement and hadn't even thought himself capable of it. But now, with the decrypted message staring back at him, he realizes that this choice may no longer be his to make.

The world outside feels so distant now, as if the city and its inhabitants are nothing more than shadows, part of the same artificial system that has kept him numb for so long. And yet, in this moment, everything feels more real than it has in years.

Welcome...

The message remains on the screen, patient and insistent, waiting for him to act.

For the first time in what feels like forever, Alex feels something stir inside him—defiance, anger, and the need to know the truth. He had spent so long buried under the weight of his own denial, convincing himself that it was easier to follow the rules, stay safe, and protect his family by staying silent.

But deep down, Alex knows that silence has only allowed the GSF to tighten its grip further. He knows that the longer he stays silent, the more he risks losing everything he loves—Jackson, Mila, and his sense of self.

He stands there for a long time, the cool night air pressing against him as he stares down at the message. The city moves on below him, unaware of the choice he's about to make, unaware of the door that has just been opened.

Welcome...

The word is a promise. No, it's more than that. It's a challenge.

Exhausted, Alex finally steps back inside. He sinks into his chair, still staring at the message as he tries to let a decision settle into him. But sleep claims him before he can make one.

Chapter 6

Hell's Mirage

The low whine of the self-driving car fills the silence as Alex stares out the window, the city blurring into a cold, metallic haze. An automated voice reminds him of his estimated arrival time at UmbraCorp, but Alex barely hears it. His mind is elsewhere—haunted by the single word that flashed on the old smartphone the night before: *Welcome...*

He's known for a while that something was coming that would pull him deeper into the undercurrent swirling beneath the polished surface of Valhalla Center. But seeing it in text, glowing on that relic of a device, made it real. Too real. His chest tightens as he tries to push the thoughts away, but they cling to him, insistent, like shadows in the corners of his vision.

The city outside is pristine, just as it always is—perfectly controlled, flawlessly designed, and utterly hollow. Drones buzz above, maintaining their constant vigilance, while automated billboards flash the latest government-approved messages, a cycle of slogans endlessly repeating. *Safety is Freedom. Order is Happiness. Progress is Control.*

The car announces their arrival at UmbraCorp. Alex steps out into the morning crowd of workers, all moving in their practiced routines toward the stark corporate world he's become so accustomed to.

A tap on his shoulder breaks through his thoughts.

"Good for a meal at 1st Street Diner," the man says in a low voice, extending his hand. He's nondescript—faded clothes and a forgettable face. Just another cog in the machine. But there's something in his eyes, a spark of recognition, that sets Alex on edge.

The man presses a small silver coin into Alex's palm before disappearing into the stream of workers without another word. Alex glances down at the coin, his brow furrowing. It's heavy for its size, cold against his skin, and etched with a symbol—an infinity sign with a small '2' above it, meaning infinity squared. Something about it feels...significant.

He slips the coin into his pocket.

Work at UmbraCorp feels more oppressive than usual today. The sterile efficiency of the office hums along as it always does, but Alex feels a weight pressing down on him with every step he takes. The endless sea of cubicles stretches before him, each identical to the last, filled with workers absorbed in their tasks, oblivious to the outside world.

But today, Alex can't shake the feeling that he's being watched—not by the drones or the cameras, but by something more...subtle. His wrist communicator buzzes with routine alerts and reminders, but he swipes them away without reading, his mind already elsewhere.

Hours pass in a blur of mindless tasks—debugging surveillance algorithms and optimizing social credit tracking systems—until, finally, his shift ends. As he walks through the corridors, his thoughts drift back to the coin—the small, seemingly harmless token now burning a hole in his pocket. Without even realizing it, his feet carry him to 1st Street Diner.

The diner is a relic, standing in sharp contrast to the sleek lines of the surrounding city. Its neon sign flickers dimly, casting a glow over the chipped paint and worn-down booths inside. It's a place that shouldn't exist in Valhalla Center, a place too imperfect to fit within the city's carefully crafted image. And yet, it's here. Waiting.

Alex pushes the door open, the chime above ringing appreciatively. The warm smell of coffee and fried food greets him, and for a moment, the tension in his chest eases. This is familiar. Real.

There's a woman sitting alone at the counter. Her sharp gaze finds him as soon as he walks in, and she gives him a small nod. He hesitates, his fingers still wrapped around the silver coin in his pocket. He walks to a booth in the corner and sits. The diner is nearly empty, which makes it all the more noticeable when the woman slides into the booth across from him.

"Hey, stranger," she says, her voice casual but her eyes keen. "You made it."

Alex tenses, studying her carefully. "Do I know you?"

"Casey West," she says, offering no handshake. "And no, you don't know me. But I know about you."

Alex glances around the diner, the tension in his shoulders never quite releasing. "What is this place?" he whispers. "And why am I here?"

She leans back, crossing her arms. "This is a hole in the wall, like a lot of places that shouldn't exist in a city like this. Perfect for people who don't want to be noticed."

Alex raises an eyebrow, but before he can respond, Casey reaches into her jacket and pulls out a coin identical to the one in his pocket. She flips it between her fingers, the silver glinting in the low light.

"So, you've got one of these," she says meeting his gaze. "It means you're starting to see things differently."

Alex takes the coin out and places it on the table between them. "What does this mean?"

"See the symbol?" Casey points to the infinity sign with its superscript two. "That's Voxx Pop's cryptocurrency logo. We use digital currency that's completely off-grid. Untraceable by the AI. It's how we survive in this city without leaving a digital trail."

Alex frowns, studying the etched symbol. "Why give out silver coins then?"

Casey smirks. "Think about what precious metals and cryptocurrency have in common. They both hold value beyond the reach of tyrants. This coin is just a symbol, but what it represents—our digital currency—keeps us free from the GSF's control. Outside their system, just like us."

Alex still doesn't fully understand how Voxx Pop operates, but he now knows that it's much more than a resistance movement. It's an entire world hidden beneath the surface of the city, invisible to the all-seeing eyes of the state.

"So, what now?" Alex asks, his voice quieter. "What's the next step?"

Casey takes a slow sip of her coffee, watching him over the rim of her cup. "The next step is seeing through the lies."

Alex leans forward, intrigued. "What lies?"

"All of them," Casey says. She sets her cup down and leans closer, her voice dropping to a conspiratorial whisper. "Look, the system isn't just about control. It's about manipulation. They're not just watching us—they're shaping the way we think, the way we react. Everything is designed to keep us compliant and from questioning the status quo."

Alex feels a chill crawl up his spine. "How do they do it?"

Casey's eyes sharpen, and her voice takes on a more serious tone. "People instinctively trust those in power, even when they shouldn't. The GSF knows that. They position themselves as protectors, the ones who keep the world from falling apart. It's all a carefully constructed image."

"And repetition," she continues, her voice gaining momentum. "If you hear a lie enough times, it starts to feel like the truth. The GSF repeats the same messages over and over—*Safety is Freedom. Order is Happiness.* They drum it into people's heads until they believe it."

Alex nods slowly, his mind racing. He's heard these messages his entire life, but now, with the fog beginning to lift, he sees them for what they really are.

"People don't like change," Casey says. "They prefer the familiar, even when the familiar is killing them. It's easier to accept the world as it is than to fight for something different. That's why so many just...comply."

Alex feels a knot tighten in his chest. "And what about automation? Everything is automated now."

"Exactly," Casey says. "People trust machines more than they trust themselves. The GSF hides behind automation, pretending that it's objective and that it can't be questioned. But that's the biggest lie of all. The system is programmed to control us."

Alex sits back, absorbing the weight of her words. Every point she makes hits with unnerving accuracy. For years, he's trusted the system—trusted the way things are—but now he sees the threads pulling it all together. And they're starting to unravel.

Casey lets the silence hang between them for a moment before she speaks again. "You're starting to see through the lies, Alex. That's why they gave you the coin."

He stares down at the silver piece in his hand, the infinity symbol and squared number etched into its surface. It feels heavier now, laden with a meaning he's only beginning to grasp.

"What's the point of all this?" he asks. "What does Voxx Pop want?"

Casey's smile is small, almost sad. "Freedom. Real freedom. Not the kind the GSF dangles in front of us like a carrot, but the kind where people aren't being manipulated, controlled, and lied to. It's not going to be easy. But we're fighting for a world where people can choose for themselves and think for themselves."

Alex exhales slowly, the weight of her words settling over him. He's spent so long in the dark, going through the motions of life in Valhalla Center, never questioning, never fighting. But now, with the coin in his hand and the truth laid bare in front of him, he feels the stirrings of something new. Something dangerous and exhilarating—a defiance that has long been buried under years of compliance.

Casey watches him carefully as though weighing his reaction. "It's a lot to take in, I know," she says, her voice softening. "But it's time for you to make a choice. You've seen the prison we live in. Now you can either keep playing by their rules, or you can do something about it."

Alex stares out the window, the city bustling just beyond the glass. The controlled landscape he's always resented stretches before him—the drones, the billboards, the perfectly engineered buildings. But now, for the first time, he sees a possibility of fighting back, of doing more than just surviving in the GSF's suffocating grip.

"And how do I know this isn't just another layer of manipulation?" Alex finally asks, his voice thick with uncertainty. "How do I know Voxx Pop is different?"

Casey leans forward, her expression deadly serious. "You don't," she says flatly. "That's the point. But the difference is we don't tell you what to believe. We give you the tools to see the truth for yourself. After that, it's up to you."

Alex mulls over her words. For years, he's been told what to do, what to think, and how to live. And now, standing on the precipice of something real, something that could shatter the illusions he's lived under, he's paralyzed by the enormity of it all.

Before he can respond, Casey reaches into her pocket and pulls out another object—a small, intricate keychain with the same infinity symbol etched into its metal surface. She spins it around her fingers, studying his reaction.

"Consider this your introduction," she says. "The coin's just a start. There's more to learn and more to see. But you need to decide if you're ready for that."

Alex grips the coin tighter, his mind racing. He's never been ready for any of this. Not the pamphlet, not the encrypted message, not even the hidden whispers that now fill his mind with questions. But if he walks away now, he knows he'll never be able to forget what he's seen. He'll never be able to unsee the cracks in the system, the lies woven into the very fabric of their lives.

He looks back at Casey, the weight of his decision settling in his chest. "So, what now?"

Casey smiles again. "Now, you take the next step. And you do it carefully. Keep your eyes open. You'll see the signs."

She rises from the booth, swiping her wrist device over the table's payment sensor as she picks up her jacket. Before she walks away, she gives Alex a long, pointed look. "And maybe you can treat me to dinner sometime."

Her words are light, playful even, but there's something more behind them. This is far from just a casual invitation. He watches her go, her figure disappearing into the dim light of the diner, and realizes she's left him with more questions than answers.

The diner feels smaller now, the walls closing in as Alex slides out of the booth and walks toward the door. His fingers are still wrapped around the coin in his pocket. Its weight feels different now; it is heavier and more real.

He pauses momentarily at the door, his mind swirling with the possibilities before him. The city beyond the diner's window gleams under the neon lights, but it no longer holds the same allure. It's a mirage, a glittering illusion designed to keep everyone distracted and complacent.

With a deep breath, Alex turns toward the counter, walking past the door instead of through it. As he approaches the front, his heart pounds.

Alex reaches into his pocket and places the silver coin on the counter, its infinity symbol catching the light. The employee looks at him, her eyes widening slightly before a knowing smile spreads across her face.

"Won't you join us for Sunday Brunch?" she asks quietly—and then retreats before Alex can answer.

Chapter 7

Plague of Memories

A lex sits alone in a dimly lit corner of his apartment, the noise of the city outside a distant murmur. His wrist communicator blinks softly on the table; the screen is dark, and its steady pulse is the only interruption in the silence. He feels the cool weight of the silver coin as it rests in his palm.

Casey's words still echo in his mind, cutting through the carefully curated facade of Valhalla Center's perfectly engineered world.

"People instinctively trust those in power, even when they shouldn't."

He hadn't fully grasped the meaning of what she'd said when she said it; it had reminded him of jargon he'd read in corporate briefings or the endless stream of UmbraCorp modules: words that meant everything and nothing at once.

But now, having had time to reflect, those words feel alive, buzzing under his skin. He can see the pattern everywhere—how easily he'd accepted UmbraCorp's security protocols because they came from authority figures. How he'd dismissed his own doubts when his coworkers nodded along with every new restriction. How he'd told himself that if the surveillance was dangerous, surely the thousands of engineers like him would have spoken out by now. The slow twisting of perceptions, the quiet erosion of independence. The GSF hasn't just controlled him; they've *molded* him.

Had he been too scared to look under the hood and see all that was going on? He isn't sure. All he knows is that with the truth starting to surface, he can't unsee it.

"People don't like change."

Alex rubs his eyes, exhaustion and nervous excitement competing for his attention. He feels like his entire worldview has been flipped on its head. For years, the constant thrum of automated systems and the relentless cycle of reminders and updates from the GSF, had been, in a strange way, reassuring—a sign that everything was under control, that life was running smoothly. But now, he feels trapped in a system that has taken everything from him, though he had never realized just how much.

The coin feels heavier as he runs his finger over its smooth cold surface. It's not just a symbol of Voxx Pop's rebellion. It's personal now. The system he's lived under hasn't just oppressed him—it has stolen the people he loves.

His hand tightens around the coin, the memories from the pandemic pressing down on him like a wave, pulling him under. As his eyelids capitulate to his fatigue, the memories are so vivid it's as if he's re-living them.

It had all started with his sister, Lila, the sweetest soul on the planet. Her laughter had always been contagious, the kind that filled a room with warmth. Alex can still hear it now, echoing in his mind, even though it's been years since that laughter was silenced.

He remembers the last time they stood together, Lila leaning against the doorway of her apartment, arms crossed, a teasing smile playing at the corners of her mouth. The world had already started to unravel—quarantines, curfews, rising death tolls—but Lila had been defiant in the face of it all.

"We'll get through this," she had said, her voice steady, reassuring. "It's just another storm, Alex. We've weathered worse."

But this storm had been different.

The virus had swept through the city like wildfire, and the hospitals were overwhelmed and overcrowded within weeks. Lila had fallen sick fast—too fast. Alex remembers the frantic phone calls, Lila gasping for air, every sentence more of a struggle. "I'm fine, baby bro," she had insisted, even as her voice broke with the effort of breathing. "I'll be out of here before you've had a chance to miss me."

But Lila never left that hospital. By the time Alex was allowed to see her, it was through a glass wall, her body barely even visible under the tangle of tubes and machines that fought to keep her alive. He had stood there with his forehead pressed against the cold window, helpless as her breathing slowed and the heart monitor beside her bed began its inevitable descent.

There had been no final words, no last moments of comfort. Just the obnoxious, metronomic beeping of a machine; when those beeps stopped, it was official: another life cut short. The memory is so sharp that even now, Alex can feel the glass against his palms and hear the way the heart monitor flatlined in that unnerving silence.

And then, there was Tim, his younger cousin. Full of life and always pushing the envelope, he was perpetually on the hunt for his next adventure. He was the kind of kid who thought he was invincible, even when the world was falling apart.

Alex had tried to warn him and begged him to be careful and listen to the officials, but Tim had always laughed it off. "It's basically just the flu, dude," he had said, a cocky grin plastered across his face. "The government's overreacting, like usual. Chill. It's gonna be fine."

The words haunt Alex now. That belief that nothing could touch him. But the virus had done more than just touch him: it'd taken him for keeps. Alex remembers the late-night phone call from the hospital, the nurse's detached voice informing him that Tim's "condition had worsened," whatever the hell that meant. The truth was that Tim had been too weak and too far gone by the time anyone realized how bad it was.

Alex's last conversation with Tim had been over a video call, the teenager's once-vibrant face jaundiced, his athletic body whittled down to a bag of bones. Even then, Tim had tried to joke about it, but his voice was barely a whisper. "Hindsight's twenty-twenty, cuz," he had rasped, forcing a smile.

And then, two days later, Tim was relegated to the past tense. Another life was lost, another victim added to the growing list of casualties that were starting to feel less like people and more like statistics. Just another number on the endless stream of reports churned out by the state.

Just another number.

Alex's eyes snap open, the memories hitting him like a bag of bricks. Lila. Tim. They'd trusted the system, trusted that the state had their best interests at heart. But now Alex sees what really went down. The pandemic wasn't just a tragedy—it was an opportunity. The GSF used it to tighten their grip, to further the narrative of control. They created an environment where fear was the coin of the realm, and compliance was the only way to survive. They didn't fail—they engineered the crisis to consolidate their power.

Stay indoors. Trust the state. We're all in this together. Keep hope alive.

The slogans had been so ubiquitous that no one thought to wonder if there was truth behind them. Alex had repeated them to himself and to his family, believing that they were the path to survival. They were the strings pulling them all into submission, keeping them just compliant enough to avoid asking the real questions.

The coin in Alex's hand feels like a lifeline, a connection to something real, something outside of the GSF's reach. It isn't just about resistance anymore—it's about justice. For Lila. For Tim. For all the expendable souls who were sacrificed to keep the machine turning.

The weight of it feels suffocating and liberating at once. For so long, he buried the pain and convinced himself that it was just part of life's cycles, that there was nothing he could do. But now, with Casey's words still echoing in his mind, Alex knows better.

His family didn't have to die. None of the hundreds of thousands who perished had to suffer like that, particularly the young. The GSF had orchestrated it all—using death and fear to tighten their control, to make people more dependent on their system. They hadn't just failed to stop it; they'd weaponized it.

Alex stands from the couch, pacing the small space of the apartment. Outside the living room window, the city churns with its usual, quiet monotony. It's a perfect facade for the truth of the control that grips every corner of the citizens' lives. The propaganda, the manipulation, the carefully orchestrated lies—it all feels so obvious now. And yet, for so long, he had accepted it and played his part in the grand illusion.

Alex turns the coin over in his hand, the infinity symbol catching the dim light. It's more than just currency. It's a reminder that there's a world beyond this—a world that the GSF can't control.

Voxx Pop isn't offering resistance. They're offering freedom.

For the first time in what feels like years, Alex feels the stirring of something beyond anger or numbness. It's an emotion that has been locked away for so long; its return feels like a triumph in and of itself. He feels *hope*.

Alex can feel the change happening inside him. It's as if the veil has been lifted, and everything is clearer now. He sees Valhalla Center for what it truly is—a prison. A prison he's been living in, blindfolded by the lies they've all been told for so long.

He's not blind anymore.

Sunday Brunch. The cryptic invitation from the diner employee plays on a loop in his brain, like a promise that there's more to come. More to see. More to understand. And Alex is ready. For the first time in a long time, he's not afraid. He's not seeing every negative possibility a mile down the road. He's ready to see what lies beyond the walls of the world he's known, ready to join the fight for something real.

The coin feels warm now, as if his energy has transferred to the small silver piece. Alex grips it tighter. He doesn't know what awaits him at Sunday Brunch, but it's damn sure more than this life has in store for him.

Chapter 8

Turning Point

Alex stares at the silver coin on the table, watching the light from his apartment window catch on its smooth surface. It glints subtly in the dim room as if it holds a secret just waiting for him to uncover it. His fingers twitch toward it, but he doesn't pick it up. Not yet. He's been sitting in the same spot for hours, his mind a whirlwind of doubt, fear, and indecision.

Join us for Sunday Brunch. The invitation was simple enough. But its implications...have grown heavier as the days have passed, and now, with the time for said brunch looming, it feels impossibly heavy. It all feels...impossible.

Since that conversation with Casey, Alex has found himself trapped in an endless cycle of contemplation, questioning every move, thought, and glance from the people around him. That would become more than a phase—it'd become his life.

Joining Voxx Pop means stepping into a world that promises resistance—revolution even—but it also means risking everything he's known and built—his family, his safety, his life. The decision weighs heavier on him with each passing moment, more complicated and tangled than ever.

To say that the GSF doesn't take kindly to dissent is an understatement. They would come for him and his family. People who oppose the system don't just disappear quietly—they're made examples of. He's seen it happen: public trials broadcast on every screen, forced confessions, families separated and relocated, their social credit scores destroyed until they can't even buy food. Their punishment is loud enough to terrify anyone left behind into submission. He'd be putting Mila and Jackson at enormous risk. Could he live with himself if his involvement in Voxx Pop brought the GSF down on their heads?

But what are they really living for? What if the system never changes? Could he continue to live like this, knowing what he knows now? *That's* the real question.

Every day since that night on the balcony, since that single word—*Welcome*—glowed on his screen, Alex has seen the system for what it truly is: a prison with glass walls designed to look like freedom.

The risks are massive, no question. They feel insurmountable at times. Even his day-to-day feels riskier now. He doesn't know if anyone there has noticed the change in him, but he knows he's walking a thin line. Each step forward feels like a misstep waiting to happen. It's like someone is watching him and waiting for him to slip.

But then there's Jackson.

Alex leans against the doorframe and watches his son, who sits cross-legged in his room, completely immersed in the VR world. The blue glow of the VR boundary casts an eerie light over Jackson's face, and Alex feels a pang of something between sadness and anger. Jackson spends more time in that virtual world than in the real one. He doesn't know his son anymore. The boy who used to ask questions and explore the world with wide-eyed curiosity has been replaced by someone disconnected from reality, seduced by the illusions of the GSF's endless entertainment and distractions.

Alex remembers the conversation they had about the "dead internet theory." Jackson laughed when Alex suggested that half his online friends might be AI bots and that the GSF could be filling the virtual world with artificial interactions to keep people isolated and controlled. Jackson brushed him off, convinced that the world inside the VR headset was just as real and valuable as the one outside. Jackson might never understand what the GSF is doing to them—to all of them. But if Alex does nothing and just watches his son disappear into a world of artificial interaction, what kind of future will Jackson have?

And then there's Mila.

She's sitting at the kitchen table, scanning her tablet, her eyes half-glazed as she reads yet another issue of The Global Progress Report, the GSF's flagship economic publication listing the benefits of the current economic model. She looks up briefly when she sees Alex, giving him a small, distracted smile, before returning to the endless stream of sanctioned information. Mila has always trusted the system. She's never questioned it, not once. In fact, she believes in it.

Alex feels guilt settle over him. Mila is a good person. She works hard, does her part, and follows the rules. She believes in the GSF's promise of safety, order, and progress. And for the most part, she's content with the life they've built. She doesn't see the cracks in the system. She doesn't feel the suffocating grip of control tightening around them with every new law, every new restriction, every new piece of propaganda.

If he joins Voxx Pop, Mila will never understand. She'll see him as reckless, putting their family at risk for something she doesn't even believe exists. She trusts the GSF, even if Alex doesn't anymore. What will happen to their relationship if he takes this step? Will she leave him? Will she take Jackson and go?

He wavers between feeling as though he owes it to them not to pursue this any further and thinking that he owes it to them to give them all a chance at something better.

The days drag on, each one more anxiety-ridden than the last, and Alex finds himself drowning in a confusion of thoughts. His mind cycles through the same thoughts and the same fears repeatedly.

The GSF is everywhere. They see everything. They're always ready to snuff out any sign of dissent. Joining Voxx Pop would be like painting a target on his back, writing "Fire Here," and walking down to see BOB, the GSF's most feared enforcer—an AI that looks and moves so human-like, you'd never know it wasn't flesh and blood until it decided to break you. He's spent his whole life protecting his family, doing whatever it takes to keep them safe. Could he really jeopardize that?

But then the loop circles back: what kind of life is he protecting? Every day, the cracks in the system become clearer, and he wonders how he viewed the world through such foggy lenses.

The endless cycle of work, of mindless compliance, of watching the world pass him by without ever feeling alive in it. That's not a life. It's certainly not freedom. And if he does nothing, Jackson will slip into the GSF's control. The virtual world is one of their greatest weapons, keeping people like his son disconnected from the real one.

Maybe joining Voxx Pop will give him a way to change things. To fight for a world where Jackson doesn't have to disappear into a headset to feel like he's living. Or at least a world where he's able to tell the difference and make that choice for himself.

He comes back to Mila, the woman who was once his ride-or-die, the person with whom he was going to change the world. The world changed before they had a chance to do that, though; they ran out of dreams before they could turn them into realities. He tells himself that he's doing this for the person Mila used to be; hell, for the person that *he* used to be. Alex knows that if he takes this step, it will drive a wedge between them. Mila will never see things the way he does. She'll never understand why he feels he needs to do this.

Somewhere, buried deep in parts of her brain that she's too scared to access, he knows that she remembers those old feelings, even just one: hope.

Alex also knows that by doing nothing and staying silent, he is slowly suffocating under the weight of a system designed to keep people like him from questioning and fighting back. He can feel the walls closing in on him, pressing down with every new law and restriction. He knows he's running out of time to make a decision.

One evening, after days of sleepless nights and endless internal debate, Alex finds himself standing on the balcony again, staring out at the city below. The distant hum of drones, the flicker of neon signs, the ever-watchful eyes of the GSF—it all feels like a web closing in around him.

The coin is in his hand again, its weight familiar and almost comforting now. Alex rolls it between his fingers, feeling the smooth edges and the cold metal. It's a simple thing, but it represents so much more. It's a choice. A decision. A commitment.

The risks are real, he tells himself again, trying to keep the fear at bay. *The consequences are real.*

But so are the rewards.

What kind of world is this? A world where his son is slipping away, piece by piece, into a manufactured reality. A world where his wife, the woman he loves, accepts every spoon-fed lie the GSF offers, never questioning or wondering what might lie beyond the walls of their pristine city.

What kind of future is this? A predictable one at best, a horrifying one at worst.

Casey's words come back to him again, cutting through his fog of doubt: *"Whatever holds value beyond the reach of tyrants is real."* Maybe the future Voxx Pop promises is real, too. A future where people can choose their own paths, where Jackson doesn't have to live with the GSF's hand constantly guiding his every thought and action. A future where Mila doesn't have to blindly trust the lies she's been told her entire life.

A world where Mila can play music again. How he misses that beautiful sound...

Alex grips the coin tighter, his pulse quickening. He knows what he has to do. He's made a list in his head of the risks and the dangers (he wouldn't dare write out a pros and cons list). And he's gone back and forth about it, sure, but for the first time in days, the choice feels clear.

He has to join Voxx Pop. Not just for himself but for Jackson, for Mila, and for the possibility of a world where they are free. Even if they don't understand it now. Hell, even if they *never* understand.

Alex turns from the balcony, and the decision is made. Sunday Brunch is coming, and with it, the next step in his journey. He pockets the coin, feeling the metal press against his skin as he steps back inside the apartment. The weight of the decision is heavy, sure, but no longer suffocating. It's a burden he's chosen to carry, and with that choice comes a strange sense of relief. The constant cycle of doubt, the endless questions swirling in his mind, finally begin to quiet.

He glances toward Jackson's room, the glow from the VR system casting long shadows on the floor. Alex wonders what Jackson would say if he knew what his father was about to do. Would he understand? Better yet, would he even care?

Alex's chest tightens, and the helplessness creeps back in. He was there once—plugged in, compliant, comfortable with the lie that the GSF had sold to everyone in Valhalla Center. And though it feels like an eternity ago, it wasn't. But now, every time he looks at Jackson, it's like watching a part of him fade away. And he won't let that happen. Not to his son. Not anymore.

Mila glances up from her tablet as Alex walks past. There's a flicker of concern in her eyes, the briefest hint of curiosity as she takes in his expression.

"Everything okay?" she asks. Her voice is casual but laced with something deeper. She can't know, can she?

Alex forces a smile, trying to push down the storm brewing inside him. "Yeah. Just...you know...thinking."

Mila nods, seemingly satisfied with his response, and returns to the screen in front of her. The silence between them is more deafening than usual, like an unspoken barrier that neither of them is willing to cross.

Will she ever take off her state-sponsored glasses and look at the world with her own eyes?

It's a question that's haunted him since he first realized how deep the GSF's control ran. Mila trusts the system so implicitly and sees it as the bedrock of their stability. How could he possibly explain that the very thing she believes in is what's keeping them imprisoned?

But whether she understands or not, Alex knows he's made his choice. He can't keep living in this gilded cage, pretending everything is fine when he knows the truth. Voxx Pop is offering a way out—not just for him but for the future of everyone in Valhalla Center. For Jackson, for Mila, for the generations to come.

It really boils down to this: if he *doesn't* take this step, if he *doesn't* fight for something better, then what kind of man is he?

He closes his eyes and takes several slow breaths, easing the tension in his body. The decision has been made. There's no turning back now. *Sunday Brunch* is the next step, the point of no return, and for the first time in what feels like years, Alex feels ready.

The days pass slowly, each one marked by an uneasy quiet as Alex prepares for what's to come. He goes to work and goes through the motions, but everything feels different now—sharper, more vivid. The glass walls of UmbraCorp feel thinner and more fragile as if the slightest pressure could shatter the entire illusion. He watches the people around him, his colleagues, and their blank faces as they march through their daily routines, never questioning or wondering. It's like watching ghosts.

He feels the distance growing between him and the life he's lived up until now. Every conversation with Mila feels hollow, every interaction with Jackson tinged with a sense of urgency that he can't quite put into words. The decision to join Voxx Pop looms over everything, a secret he carries with him like a weight that's both heavy and freeing at the same time.

Sunday approaches, and with it, the promise of something new. Something real.

At breakfast the following day, Alex switches off the AI-tuned television. It resists, flashing a message about "optimal viewing conditions" before going dark.

"Viewer satisfaction will decrease by sixty-three percent," the AI warns.

"Good," Alex mutters, turning to the kitchen where the food synthesizer is already humming to life, its display showing the morning's nutrient-optimized menu options.

"Would you like me to synthesize your standard breakfast selection?" the AI asks.

"No," Alex interrupts, pulling out actual cooking implements from a rarely-used cabinet. "I'm making real food today."

He catches Mila's surprised look as she enters the kitchen. "Is something wrong with the synthesizer?"

"Nothing's wrong," he says, measuring flour he's specially ordered—at a premium—from one of the few remaining natural food suppliers. "Just tired of synthetic food."

The waffles come out slightly burnt, the eggs over-scrambled, but they smell like actual food—not the artificially perfected aroma the synthesizer produces. Jackson pokes at his waffle with his fork, frowning at the darkened edges.

"The synthesizer never burns anything," he points out.

"No, it doesn't," Alex agrees, sitting down with his own plate. "But this is real food, not synthetic nutrients shaped to look like waffles."

Mila and Jackson exchange glances as they eat, not used to seeing him cook, not when the food synthesizer could prepare perfectly calibrated nutrient portions. The synthesizer sits dormant, its status light pulsing disapprovingly.

But today feels different. Today, he wants something authentic, even if it's flawed. Even if it means paying extra for real ingredients and enduring his family's confused looks.

"This tastes...different," Jackson admits finally, taking another bite of his burnt waffle. "More... real. It's actually kind of good."

Alex smiles, watching his son eat non-synthetic food for the first time in years. "Yeah," he says. "It is."

The night before Sunday Brunch, Alex stands on the balcony once more, the city sprawling beneath him in all its engineered perfection. The drones buzz in the distance, and the neon signs flicker with the same empty messages, the warnings of compliance. They're designed to spike fear, to question what you're about to do if what you're thinking of doing would harm the state.

But tonight, Alex isn't afraid. He isn't filled with the same dread that has haunted him for so long. He's ready to step into the unknown, to take the risk, because he knows that what awaits him at Voxx Pop could be the key to breaking free from this prison.

As he turns back toward the apartment, he catches a glimpse of Jackson's room, the blue glow of the VR headset still flickering from beneath the door. Alex's heart aches with a deep, painful pull that threatens to break him. He doesn't know if he'll ever be able to pull Jackson back from the world the GSF has created for him, but he has to try. He owes him that much.

And for Mila—for her blind trust in the system that has kept them all imprisoned—he hopes that one day she'll see what he sees. That she'll understand why he's doing this. Maybe not today, maybe not tomorrow, but someday.

With the coin in his pocket, Alex closes the balcony door behind him, a sense of finality settling over him.

Tomorrow is Sunday Brunch. Tomorrow, everything changes.

Chapter 9

Food for Thought

Alex pauses at the entrance of 1st Street Diner, his hand hovering over the door handle. A sign reads "Private Party," and something about how it's displayed seems deliberate and meaningful. He takes a deep breath and pushes the door open.

The scent of freshly brewed coffee and the chatter of quiet conversations fill the air as Alex steps inside. It's nothing like the first time he walked in. Back then, it had been a relic—a forgotten corner of Valhalla Center, its neon sign flickering like an afterthought, its patrons scarce and weary. Today, the diner is bustling with activity in a way that feels...alive.

Alex notices subtle glances and nods exchanged between patrons. He spots Casey behind the counter, and when their eyes meet, she gestures discreetly toward a door marked "Staff Only" at the back of the diner.

Following her signal, Alex makes his way through the door. Beyond it lies a large storage room, converted into what appears to be a meeting space. Here, hidden from public view, the tables are full of people—some leaning in close, whispering in urgent tones, others scanning encrypted devices, their eyes flicking across the screens with intense focus. The air crackles with an undercurrent of anticipation. Alex feels it in his bones, a low hum of something just beneath the surface. He's part of it now. *This* is what it looks like—Voxx Pop's resistance, the hidden pulse beneath the shiny surface of the city.

He scans the room and sees Casey go to the far end of the room, her formerly calm demeanor tempered by something more serious today. She catches his eye and gives him a slight nod, motioning for him to join her at the back of the room where a group of recruits—presumably his new allies—are gathering.

Alex takes a seat among them, his mind still buzzing. The voices around him rise and fall, hushed but urgent like they're all on the cusp of something big—or the edge of something dangerous. Can they tell the difference? Can he?

His heart races as he glances around, recognizing a few faces from UmbraCorp. Each person wears the same look of determination, a kind of quiet rebellion that simmers just below the surface.

At the head of the room, Casey steps forward, commanding the group's attention with that steady presence and no-nonsense bearing. The conversations die down as she reaches into a bag at her side, pulling out small, black devices and strange-looking glasses.

"These," she says, holding up one of the devices, "are encrypted communication units. 100% untraceable by the GSF's surveillance networks, even their newest iterations. They are your lifeline from here on out. Remember that. Keep them safe and use them wisely."

She moves through the room, distributing the devices. When she reaches Alex, she meets his eyes with a knowing smile, placing the unit in his hand. It's cool, compact, and weighty, with promise. His fingers curl around it, and for a moment, he feels the rush of something dangerous, something *real*. It makes no difference if it's a tool for rebellion or an organic carrot; he's missed that feeling.

"First rule of resistance," Casey says, "is don't die."

"*That's* rule number one?" Alex asks with a hint of a smile. "I was expecting something more philosophical."

"Hey, you'd be amazed how many people forget that one." She grins. "Which is why these units are your lifeline from here on out. Keep them safe and use them wisely."

Casey continues making the rounds, handing out the glasses this time. They're ultra-high-tech, to the point that they look almost alien in design. "These are facial-recognition-distorting glasses. Put them on, and the GSF's drones won't be able to track you. Wear them when you're moving through high-surveillance zones. And, the same deal: keep them safe and use them wisely. If you get caught with these, I don't need to tell you what happens."

Alex slips the glasses on, the lenses casting a slight tint over his vision. The world shifts, the edges of the diner blurring just enough to make everything feel slightly surreal. He reaches up, adjusting them, already imagining the moments when he'll need them—the dark alleys, the watchful drones overhead.

Casey isn't done yet. She crouches down, pulling out a pair of thin shoe inserts, by the looks of them.

"These," she says, tossing a pair to Alex, "are gait-recognition disruptors. Yeah, I'll bet some of you didn't even know they tracked our gaits. Each one of us has a slightly different walking pattern. Slip them into your shoes, though, and the city's tracking systems won't be able to pinpoint your movement patterns. You'll be ghosts."

Alex studies the inserts for a moment, marveling at the simplicity of the design. But the implications are profound. Every step he takes in the city could be monitored and tracked by the GSF's algorithms. But with these...he's invisible.

Once everyone is equipped, Casey steps back to the front of the room, her eyes sweeping over the group. "This is the beginning," she says. Her voice is calm but charged with meaning. "In the coming months, you'll undergo training—rigorous, demanding, and, if I'm being honest, really freakin' dangerous. But so are they! And the skills you'll learn won't just be helpful. They will be *essential*. We're not just here to survive. We're doing what people used to do: we're *building* something. A future."

The room buzzes with excitement and nerves as she continues, outlining the areas they'll cover. "You'll learn to grow your own food, hack the AI systems, and repair the old tech we've been able to salvage. We don't need their supply chains. We don't need their surveillance. We don't need their permission to live!"

Cheers ping-pong around the room. Alex stifles a smile, amazed at how gifted an orator this woman is. If he didn't know better, he'd think she was a politician. In a way, though, she is—the leader of the rebellion party.

***

Alex pauses to catch his breath inside the rooftop shed, leaning against one of the concrete planters. From the outside, the structure appears to be abandoned maintenance housing, but inside, it's a sanctuary of growth. The air is humid, carrying the scent of damp soil and fresh greenery. UV lamps line the ceiling, bathing the room in artificial sunlight and nourishing the various plants growing in plastic tubs. Metal pipes snake along the walls and between the rows, feeding water and nutrients into the vibrant green plants. It's a striking contrast to the concrete jungle visible through the shed's grimy windows—a splash of life among the gray monotony, safely concealed from the drones that patrol the city's skies.

A few other recruits are already hard at work, their hands deep in the soil or adjusting the hydroponic system's tubing. Casey moves between them, explaining the mechanics of the operation. "This isn't just about growing food," she says, kneeling beside one of the tubs to inspect a tomato plant. "It's about independence. The GSF controls the food supply, just like always. But we control this. They can't touch this."

Alex crouches beside her, watching as she lifts the delicate vine, showing him the balance of water and nutrients being fed into the plant. It's all so precise and scientific, even in its rawness. He's never thought about food like this before. To him, food has always just kind of...been there. But as he watches the plants grow and feels the warmth of the soil in his hands, he understands—this is survival. *Real* survival.

"You'll need to learn how to keep this going," Casey says, straightening up and wiping the dirt from her hands. "We're talking rooftop farming, urban gardens, vertical hydroponics—anywhere we can grow, we will. And when the system collapses—not if, but when—we'll be the ones still standing." A few murmurs of agreement ripple through the group.

Later, Alex's hands are stained from the soil as he gently transfers a row of seedlings into the tubs. There's a sense of purpose here, something he hasn't felt in years. The plants in his hands are fragile, but they're *real*—living, growing. They're more than food; they're a symbol. A reminder that there is life beyond the GSF's reach, beyond the sterile walls of Valhalla Center.

He catches a glimpse of another recruit adjusting the nutrient levels in the water flowing through the system. Their eyes meet for a moment, and in that shared look, there's understanding. They're building something here—something that can't be controlled, something that can't be taken away.

***

The room is dark, lit only by the glow of computer screens, casting an eerie blue light over the faces of the recruits. Alex's fingers hover above the keyboard, his eyes scanning lines of code that seem to blur together. The air is thick with concentration, and the fans of the computers are the only sound as they work to crack the encrypted files displayed on their screens.

Casey's voice cuts through the silence, "The GSF thinks it owns the digital space," she says, pacing behind them with her hands folded behind her back. "But remember—tech can enslave, and it can liberate. We're going to teach you how to make it do both."

Alex leans closer to the screen, his mind racing as he runs the sequence again, trying to bypass the AI's security protocols. Every keystroke feels like an act of defiance. It's a battle against the system that's been watching him for so long. He never imagined he'd be on this side of the fight—working to *break* the system instead of supporting it.

Suddenly, the lines of code shift, and a new sequence opens up in front of him. His heart skips a beat. He's in. The encrypted files open, revealing a hidden communication channel—one Voxx Pop has been trying to tap into for weeks. Alex exhales slowly as a small, triumphant smile pulls at his lips.

Next to him, another recruit lets out a quiet whoop, having just cracked a different firewall. Casey nods approvingly, her sharp eyes flicking over the screens. "You'll need these skills to build secret networks, communicate without detection, and access the information they think is untouchable. Every piece of data is a weapon. Don't forget that."

Alex rakes a hand over his face before moving to test another set of commands. The thrill of it pulses through him—this is liberation, line by line, code by code.

***

The air smells of grease and metal, the clanking of old machinery filling the space as Alex watches a fellow recruit hammer away at a rusted gear. They're deep in one of Voxx Pop's underground workshops, a hidden bunker filled with old tech salvaged from the city's scrap yards by "friendlies," Voxx Pop's term for sympathizers. Engines and generators lie in pieces along the workbenches.

Casey stands at the center of the workshop, her sleeves rolled up and oil smeared across her hands as she works alongside them. "The GSF wants you to think everything they create is indispensable," she says, wiping her hands on a rag before picking up a wrench. "They want you to believe that without their tech, you can't survive. But we know that's BS. And, the irony of it all? The machines they've abandoned and the tech they've cast aside—*that's* our key to independence. We're going to repurpose, rebuild, and reclaim everything they deemed "obsolete." These old machines will be the backbone of our self-sustaining communities."

Alex watches as Casey sets to work on an engine that looks like it hasn't run in decades. She's focused and determined, her hands moving with practiced precision. The other recruits gather around her, some kneeling by the engine, others inspecting various tools and parts scattered around the workshop.

Alex kneels beside a partially disassembled generator, its wires are frayed and the casing is rusted. He picks up a screwdriver, unsure of where to begin, but eager to try. It's been years since he's held anything so tangible—his life at UmbraCorp was dominated by sterile, digital tasks, abstract work that felt disconnected from reality.

A recruit beside him wipes oil from his hands and grins. "You ever think we'd be doing this? Getting our hands dirty instead of sitting behind a desk?"

Alex chuckles, shaking his head. "Not in a million years."

Together, they start unscrewing the casing, pulling apart the rusted pieces, and laying them out on the floor. The machinery is old but not beyond repair. Alex carefully pries open a compartment, revealing a tangled mess of wires. His brow furrows as he inspects it, trying to make sense of the worn circuits.

"Don't worry," says another recruit, a woman named Talia, who's been working with Voxx Pop longer than most. She leans over, pointing to a corroded wire. "That's your problem. Replace this, rewire it through the alternator, and you should get this thing running again."

Alex issues a nod of gratitude. They all work in silence for a while, the sounds of clinking metal and low voices filling the space. Bit by bit, the broken generator starts to come back together. With Talia's help, Alex replaces the faulty wires, tightens the loose bolts, and wipes away layers of grime that have accumulated over the years.

Finally, after hours of trial and error, the generator grumbles to life, its soft, rhythmic sound filling the workshop. Alex stares at it while a sense of accomplishment swells in his chest. It's a small victory but a significant one. Every machine they fix and every piece of tech they salvage brings them one step closer to freedom from the GSF's chokehold on technology and resources.

Casey glances over at Alex, her expression unreadable, but there's approval in her eyes. "Good work," she says, then turns back to the engine she's been working on. "We don't need their infrastructure, people! We build our own."

Over the next few weeks, Alex develops a new routine. He leaves home an hour earlier each morning, telling Mila he needs to catch up on work before the office gets busy. He spends that time in the rooftop gardens with other recruits, tending to crops that will one day sustain them. After his regular workday at UmbraCorp, he uses "system updates" and "overtime" as excuses to spend another hour with the recruits learning to hack into databases the GSF thought were untouchable. Some evenings, he tells Mila he's working late-shift maintenance while he's actually in the workshop repairing generators, engines, and old machines the state deems obsolete.

The juggling act is exhausting but necessary. Each day is a careful balance between maintaining his cover at work, appearing normal to Mila, and absorbing everything Voxx Pop can teach him. His hands are stained with soil and oil, and his mind is sharper as he learns to navigate the digital landscape of code and encryption. The fear of discovery that once gnawed at him is still there, lurking in the background, but now it's tempered by something stronger: purpose.

***

One morning, Alex is deep in the rooftop garden, his fingers gently guiding the thin roots of a hydroponic lettuce plant into place. Sweat drips down his back, but he doesn't mind. There's something about growing food—real food—that feels…grounding. Like he's taking back control one plant at a time.

"Careful with that one," Talia says, appearing at his side. She points to a spot where he's overwatered, and a small pool of nutrient-rich water is gathering at the base of the plant. "You don't want to give it too much water."

"Or what?" Alex says lightly. "The plants stage a protest?"

Talia snorts. "Worse. They drown. Then we're stuck eating whatever the synthesizer's pretending is a vegetable."

Alex winces slightly and adjusts the flow until the water recedes. "Point taken. No pressure or anything."

Talia grins, giving him a quick pat on the shoulder. "You'll get the hang of it," she says, crouching to check another row of plants.

They've all had their failures—plants that wilted from too much light, others that drowned from overwatering—but each mistake is a lesson, and each success brings them closer to self-sufficiency.

A few of the other recruits are building a new vertical garden, metal scaffolding rising from the concrete as they carefully place rows of plants in stacked containers. The setup is impressive, a testament to the ingenuity that Voxx Pop fosters in every aspect of their rebellion.

Casey walks between the rows of plants, inspecting their work. "This is how we win," she says. "Not just by hacking their systems or dismantling their machines, but by building our own way of life. One they can't touch. One they can't destroy."

Alex looks down at the small plant in his hands, marveling at its simplicity: a living thing growing right in front of him.

In the following weeks, Alex learns more than just the technical skills required to survive outside the system—he learns the value of community and working together toward a shared goal. The recruits, once strangers, begin to form bonds forged by the intensity of their mission. They are not just training to escape; they are training to build something new.

Alex's initial doubts begin to fade. The weight of his decision to join Voxx Pop still lingers, but now it feels less like a burden and more like a responsibility—a duty to those who are too blind or too scared to see the truth. He's not just doing this for himself anymore. He's doing it for Jackson, Mila, and the countless people trapped inside the GSF's web of control. And with each new skill he masters, with every plant he grows, every line of code he cracks, every machine he rebuilds, the system's grip on him weakens.

They are not just surviving. They are preparing. And the GSF has no idea what's coming.

Chapter 10

False Equivalence

Alex sits on the couch, the ever-present sound of the air filtration system filling the silence. Through Jackson's door, the blue glow of his VR boundary flickers—another night lost to the virtual world. Mila sits across from Alex, absorbed in her tablet, likely reviewing work reports. The quiet homeliness of the scene feels both familiar and somehow false.

Alex rises from the couch and grabs his jacket. "I'm heading out," he says, sliding his arms into the sleeves.

Mila looks up from her tablet, her expression a mixture of curiosity and suspicion. "Again? That's the third time this week."

He's careful not to meet her gaze as he checks the time on his wrist communicator, which he'll soon deactivate. Casey and Voxx Pop have made him feel a sense of pride again, but they've also spiked his paranoia. "Yeah, just meeting up with some friends. No big deal."

The words feel strange on his tongue, a half-truth that still tastes bitter. He's meeting the Voxx Pop recruits, not his usual colleagues or old friends from UmbraCorp. But calling them 'friends' makes it easier to navigate the secrecy that has begun to seep into his life. Makes it easier to keep Mila from asking the questions he's not ready to answer.

Mila steps forward, her eyes narrowing slightly. "You've been 'meeting friends' a lot lately."

There's a real edge to her voice now. He knows she's starting to notice the changes: the late nights, the mysterious new friends, the quiet conversations that end with vague explanations. He can sense her unease and how it creeps into her words, into the silences that fill the space between them.

Or, in times like these, he doesn't have to sense anything; she's playing her concern at maximum volume.

Still, he forces a smile, slipping into the role he's played for years—the compliant husband and the voice of reason. "You know how it is," he says with a shrug. "Work's been intense, and honestly, babe, I just need a break. Blow off steam. Catch up with the guys."

Mila doesn't move. Her arms remain crossed, her gaze fixed on him. "Blowing off steam," she echoes. There's a pause, and when she speaks again, there's a tremor of uncertainty beneath her words. "Are you sure everything's okay, Alex? You've seemed...different lately."

Alex stiffens, his mind racing for a way out of the conversation. He can feel the walls closing in, the truth pressing against his chest, but he can't let it slip. Not yet. Instead, he reaches for something familiar, something that has always worked in the past—a tactic the GSF has perfected over the years: deflection.

He puts his hands on her shoulders and adopts the tone he knows will put her at ease. "Mila," he says, "you worry when I'm too quiet. You worry when I'm too secluded. Now you worry because I want to see friends. Everything's fine. You know how things are these days—everyone's stressed and juggling a million things at once. It's just the world we live in now."

It's a carefully crafted response, a blend of reassurance and dismissal that's meant to quell her suspicions without actually addressing them. Mila's expression falters, her arms loosening at her sides as she considers his words.

But then she frowns. "I guess...it just feels like you've been saying that a lot lately. Everything's fine, just the way things are...I don't know, Alex. It's starting to feel like..."

"Like what?" Alex asks. He doesn't want her digging too deep.

She opens her mouth to respond but hesitates, seemingly wrestling with her thoughts. "I know you're not lying to me," she says, shaking her head. "And I don't want to make a big deal out of nothing. But think of how it sounds. Think of what it's like for me to suddenly see you like this, all..."

"What? Happy? Excited about something? Wanting to do more? That's not something bad, babe. It's a *good* thing."

"You promise me that I have nothing to worry about?"

Alex places a hand on her arm in what he hopes is a reassuring gesture. "I promise you there's nothing to worry about. We've got enough going on without inventing problems, right? Trust me."

The phrases slip from his mouth easily, almost too easily. They're the same lines he's heard a hundred times on the media broadcasts, the same carefully constructed reassurances designed to keep people compliant and to keep them from questioning. And he can see it in Mila's eyes—the way she's torn between the comfort those words offer and the creeping suspicion that something isn't quite right. The same words that soothe her when they come from the media now leave her unsettled when they come from him.

Mila bites her lip, still standing there, not quite ready to let the conversation die. "You sound like one of those news reports," she says, almost teasing but with an undercurrent of worry. "You know, the ones where everything's fine, don't ask questions, just keep moving forward..."

Alex's pulse quickens. She's closer to the truth than she realizes, and for a split second, he wonders if she'll push harder and if she'll see through the veneer he's trying to maintain. But before she can say more, he leans in and kisses her cheek, letting his touch serve as a distraction, a way to cut the conversation short.

"Relax," he whispers, pushing a stray hair from her face. "I'll be home before you know it."

Mila's face softens under his touch, but there's still a flicker of doubt in her eyes. She nods slowly, stepping back as Alex pulls away. "Okay," she says quietly. "Just...be careful."

"I always am," he says with a smile, though the weight of his words settles uneasily in his chest.

As Alex makes his way toward the door, he can still feel Mila's eyes on him, a heavy presence that lingers long after he's left the apartment. The hallway outside feels colder than usual. The fluorescent lights overhead cast a sterile glow on the polished floors. He shoves his hands into his jacket pockets, his fingers brushing against the encrypted device Voxx Pop gave him. It feels heavier than before like it's absorbing the tension that buzzes under his skin.

He tries to shake it off, focusing on the task ahead.

But Mila's face keeps creeping into his mind. The way she looked at him, the flicker of doubt in her eyes, the way she had almost—almost—seen through his deflections. She's never questioned him like that before. Not really. Sure, they've had disagreements, but this felt different.

What troubles him most is how easily he fell into using GSF's tactics. The very methods he's fighting against.

Everything's fine. Don't make a big deal out of nothing. Trust the system.

Empty phrases designed to shut down questions and maintain control. He became the very thing he despises, manipulating Mila's trust just as the GSF manipulates the masses.

The irony isn't lost on him. Here he is, part of a resistance movement fighting against oppression and control, yet he's using the same psychological tactics to keep Mila in the dark. He can now see how easy it is to fall into that trap, to justify manipulation for a greater cause. It had worked, for the most part. Mila hadn't pushed further. But something about her unease still lingers, and he wonders how long it will be before she starts asking questions he can't answer—and whether he's becoming part of the problem he's trying to solve.

The streets outside are quiet as Alex makes his way toward the rendezvous point. His mind is still racing, replaying the conversation with Mila, dissecting each word, each glance. He knows she trusts the system, that she believes in the GSF's promises of safety and order. She's accepted it all her life, just like he had—until recently. But now, he can't stop thinking about the cracks in that system, the lies hidden beneath the surface.

He stops at a crosswalk, waiting for the light to change, and watches as a drone hovers overhead, its lens sweeping across the street like an all-seeing eye. The people around him barely notice. Their faces are blank, and their steps are automatic. They don't question it. They don't wonder what the drone is doing or why. It's just part of life.

Alex slips the Voxx Pop glasses over his eyes, the tinted lenses distorting his face from the drones' facial-recognition software. He takes a deep breath, feeling the cool air fill his lungs. He's in the system, but not *of* it. Not anymore.

As the light turns green, he steps forward, his mind still buzzing with thoughts of Mila. She accepts the drones, the surveillance, and the constant monitoring, just as she accepts the endless stream of media reports that promise safety, security, and progress. It has never occurred to her to question it or wonder if there is another way.

But hearing those same words from him, her husband—*that* had made her uneasy. She sensed the falseness in them and the way they masked something deeper and darker. But she couldn't quite place why. Alex wonders if that moment of doubt will grow, if it will fester in the back of her mind like a seed planted by accident. Or will she dismiss it, the way she dismisses any thought that challenges the status quo?

He shakes his head, pushing the thought away. He can't worry about Mila right now. He has to stay focused. The people at Voxx Pop are counting on him. And besides, if this all works—if Voxx Pop really is the key to changing the system—then he'll be doing this for her too, even if she doesn't realize it yet. For Jackson, for Mila, and for the people too deep in the system to see the walls closing in on them. If he can help dismantle the GSF's control, maybe one day Mila will understand. Maybe she'll look back and see that he was trying to build a better future for them all.

Alex's pace quickens as he approaches the meeting point. The familiar outline of the 1st Street Diner comes into view, its neon sign flickering slightly in the twilight. The diner, once just a forgotten relic of the past, now feels like a beacon of hope. A place where the cracks in the system are acknowledged and where people like him can finally push back.

He steps inside, greeted by the low murmur of conversation. The air feels different today—charged, expectant. A few familiar faces from the Voxx Pop recruits glance up at him as he enters, nodding in recognition. It's a silent acknowledgment that they're all in this together now. No turning back.

Casey stands at the head of the room, her usual confident presence commanding attention. She's talking quietly with a few of the others, her eyes flicking toward Alex as he approaches.

"You made it," she says with a small smile, nodding toward an empty seat. "Take a seat. We're just about to start."

Alex slips into the seat, still trying to push thoughts of Mila from his mind, though they linger in the background. He knows that his absence tonight will only deepen her suspicions, but he has to keep moving forward. This is bigger than the unease brewing in their apartment. Bigger than their marriage, even. It's about the future they all deserve, even if Mila can't see it yet.

Casey turns to the group, her voice cutting through the chatter. "Tonight, we're diving deeper. No more small steps. The GSF's control runs deeper than most people realize, and we need to be ready for what's coming. That means understanding how they manipulate and use people's trust in authority and the media to control them. And it means learning to recognize those tactics in ourselves."

She pauses, scanning the room, her gaze sharp as it lands on each recruit. "Some of you have already experienced this firsthand. The system relies on logical fallacies and cognitive shortcuts to maintain its grip. People hear the same phrases and the same comforting lies repeated over and over again, and they stop questioning. They accept the false equivalencies—like when the GSF claims that questioning their control means wanting chaos, or that giving up privacy is the only way to ensure safety. They fall for the appeal to authority, believing something just because an expert or official says it's true. And they accept the endless loop of 'it could be worse' to justify not making things better.Things are *better* than they used to be, so they must be good enough. But they're not. And they never will be."

Alex feels a chill run down his spine. The words hit uncomfortably close to home. He thinks of the conversation with Mila, the way he had parroted those same comforting lies to silence her, to keep her from asking too many questions. *You're worrying too much. Everything's fine. This is just how things are.*

Casey continues. "We can't fall into the same traps. The GSF wants us to doubt ourselves and believe that any rebellion, any resistance, is pointless. They want us to believe that *they* are the only ones who can provide safety, security, and order. But that's a lie. We've already started proving it's a lie."

She steps back, motioning toward a screen behind her, which flickers to life with a map of Valhalla Center. "We've been working on key areas—disrupting their surveillance networks, rerouting communication channels, and creating safe spaces for our community to grow. The more we push back, the more we reveal just how fragile their system really is."

The recruits around Alex lean in, their eyes glued to the screen. The map is filled with red and green points, each representing a different sector of the city. Alex recognizes a few key locations—UmbraCorp, the residential zones, and the agricultural districts. But it's the smaller, lesser-known areas that catch his attention. These are the hidden pockets of resistance, the places where Voxx Pop has been quietly undermining the GSF's control.

Casey taps one of the green points on the map, bringing up a list of encrypted communication nodes. "These are ours now," she says. "They're small victories, sure, but we're accumulating assets and developing skills; that's all we can do. Make no mistake: every node we take back is another step toward dismantling the GSF's infrastructure. It's only a matter of time before we hit something big. When that happens, we need to be ready. And we will be."

Alex's pulse quickens as he takes it all in. The scale of what Voxx Pop is doing—the sheer scope of it—feels overwhelming but exhilarating at the same time. This isn't just some fringe group of rebels throwing stones at a giant. This is a coordinated effort, a strategy to slowly pull the system apart at its seams. And he's part of it now.

Casey looks around the room, her expression unreadable, but there's a fierceness in her eyes that Alex hasn't seen before. "Tonight, we'll be going over your roles. Each of you has a specific part to play in what's coming next. The GSF is going to start noticing us more, and when they do, they'll come after us hard. We need to be faster, smarter, and more united than they are."

Alex feels the weight of the coin in his pocket again. Another reminder of the choice he's made and the commitment he's already given. But as he listens to Casey outline the next steps, he can't shake the feeling that something bigger is looming on the horizon.

***

Hours later, when Alex finally makes his way back home, the city is quieter than usual, and the streets are empty, save for the occasional passing drone. The cool night air fills his lungs as he walks, his mind still buzzing with everything Casey has shared.

He slips into the apartment as quietly as possible, hoping not to wake Mila. But as soon as he steps through the door, he knows she's been waiting. She's sitting on the couch, her tablet discarded on the table in front of her, her eyes wide and wary.

"Hey," Alex says, trying to sound casual, though the guilt is already creeping in.

Mila looks up at him, her expression unreadable. For a moment, the silence hangs between them, thick and uncomfortable.

"Did you have fun?" she asks, her tone neutral but her gaze sharp.

Alex swallows, nodding. "Yeah. Thanks."

She doesn't respond right away, her eyes scanning his face as if she's searching for something—some sign of the truth he's keeping from her.

"You were gone a long time," Mila says quietly. "I really don't want to make this into something it isn't, Alex, but—"

"But what?! If you don't want to make it into something it's not, then don't!"

"What has gotten into you? You're not...you're not *you*. You'd tell me if something was wrong, wouldn't you?"

Alex forces a smile, but it feels hollow, even to him. "I'm fine, Mila. I told you, things are just hectic right now."

She nods slowly, but her eyes tell a different story. She doesn't believe him. Not fully. But she doesn't push.

As he heads to bed, Alex can't help but wonder how long he can keep this up. How long before the cracks in his lies start to show? How long before Mila stops accepting the empty reassurances and starts asking the questions he's not ready to answer?

For now, she's still in the dark. But that darkness is growing, and it'll swallow them both if she isn't brought to the light soon.

Not yet, though. Not just yet.

Chapter 11

Brains and Brawn

The 1st Street Diner is busy and full of people, and Alex can feel the tension in the air. He slips into his usual seat near the back of the back room, eyes scanning the room as the recruits gather. There's a sense of anticipation tonight, a quiet urgency that's grown stronger with each passing meeting.

They've made big strides in their training, but the stakes are rising. The world outside feels more fragile, the system's grip tightening as Voxx Pop continues its quiet rebellion.

Casey stands at the front, already engaged in quiet conversation with a group of core leaders. Her voice is low but sharp, cutting through the murmur of the crowd. Alex's attention shifts, and across the room, he spots the mysterious stranger again—the same man who had handed him the pamphlet all those weeks ago. The man leans against the wall, arms crossed, his sharp eyes sweeping over the group.

There's something magnetic about the guy, an aura of quiet confidence that's impossible to fake. The recruits have formed an unspoken bond, a recognition of shared purpose, but the man remains a mystery, his past a shadow Alex can't quite reach.

Their eyes meet briefly, and the stranger gives him a small nod. Alex nods back, feeling that same pull of curiosity. He doesn't have time to dwell on it, though—Casey claps her hands, drawing the room's attention.

"All right, everyone," she says. "Let's get started."

The conversations die down as Casey begins handing out assignments, her sharp gaze moving over the group. She glances toward the stranger, her lips curling into a teasing grin.

"Think you're ready for round two?" she asks. Her tone is playful but with a hint of challenge.

The stranger chuckles, pushing off the wall as he steps toward her. "No, no, no," he replies, grinning. "Once was enough. Thank you, though."

A ripple of laughter moves through the recruits, easing some of the tension in the room. Alex watches the exchange with interest, feeling a pang of curiosity about the relationship between them. There's history here, something deeper than just their roles in Voxx Pop. The way they banter, the way they move around each other—it's the familiarity of old friends who talk easily and move in sync.

Old friends. That's who he's with right now. They may be new friends to him, but still...that eases his guilt at lying to Mila, even just a little.

Casey grins, giving him a playful jab to the arm before addressing the group again. "This guy," she says, nodding toward the stranger, "has been with us longer than most. Knows how to handle himself in a fight."

The stranger shrugs, offering a wry smile. "Mostly from learning the hard way."

Casey's expression softens, but there's still a fire in her eyes as she turns back to the group. "Enough talk. Time to get to work. Tonight's about defense—both physical and digital. And by the end of this session, I expect every one of you to be better prepared than when you walked in. That's all I can ask and all I can expect."

Chairs scrape against the floor as the recruits push them back, making space in the middle of the back room of the diner. Casey steps into the center, her eyes gleaming with intensity. "Let's start with physical self-defense," she says, motioning for the stranger to join her. "Because if you think the GSF's enforcers won't come for you, you're not paying attention."

The stranger sighs dramatically, stepping into the circle with a grin. "Fine, but don't go easy on me just because we're friends."

Casey raises an eyebrow and stifles laughter.

What follows is a blur of movement. The two of them circle each other, bodies coiled, ready to strike. The stranger throws the first punch, but Casey deflects it effortlessly, spinning around to land a sharp jab to his side. He grunts but counters quickly, catching her wrist and twisting, only for her to slip out of his grip and drop into a low stance.

Alex watches, eyes wide, as they move with practiced precision, each strike calculated, each block a tactical maneuver. It's like watching two machines locked in a deadly dance, but with a fluidity that speaks to years of experience.

"Notice how they never waste a move," Talia whispers to Alex, nodding toward the fight. "Every strike is intentional, every step measured. You have to be efficient. The enforcers can miss a hundred times. We can't miss once."

The sparring match continues, a flurry of punches, kicks, and counterattacks until Casey lands a swift blow that knocks the stranger off-balance. He raises his hands in surrender, grinning through the defeat. "Uncle, uncle. I mean, Aunt!"

Casey smirks, stepping back as the recruits clap softly. "Lesson one," she says, addressing the group. "You don't need to be stronger but you *do* need to be smarter. AI enforcers follow programmed patterns, right? Learn their weaknesses, and you can exploit them, just like they exploit us."

The group breaks into pairs to practice the moves, and Alex finds himself partnered with the stranger. They move carefully at first, practicing the basic strikes and blocks Casey demonstrated. The stranger's movements are smooth and deliberate. Alex can't help but feel a surge of admiration.

"You're gettin' it," the stranger says, stepping back to observe Alex's form. "But don't hesitate. Commit to your strikes. Swift and decisive."

Alex nods, focusing as they run through the moves again, this time with more speed. Each block and punch feels more fluid and natural this time. His muscles burn, but it's that good kind of burn—the kind that tells him his muscles were broken down and came back stronger. *He* is stronger.

But the lesson doesn't stop there. Once the physical training winds down, Casey shifts the focus to digital self-defense. The group gathers around the tables again, their encrypted devices in hand, as Casey pulls up a holographic interface.

"In the digital world," she says, "you're just as vulnerable as you are on the streets. The GSF is watching, tracking every move, and monitoring your communications. If you don't know how to protect yourself, you're a target."

She walks them through the basics of encryption, showing them how to mask their digital footprint, how to reroute signals, and how to build firewalls that can withstand AI attacks. What surprises Alex most is how vulnerable these systems actually are.

"The GSF's real security isn't in their code," Casey explains, her voice tinged with irony. "It's in making people believe rebellion is impossible. Most of their systems are actually quite basic because they never expected anyone to try breaking in."

Beside him, the stranger leans in, offering quiet tips on how to bypass security protocols. "Don't just follow the rules," he says, smirking. "Break them. The GSF's AI is smart, but it's predictable. They never programmed it to look for people thinking independently."

Alex nods, feeling a rush of adrenaline as he cracks into a secure communication channel without triggering the alarms. The more he learns, the more he realizes the truth—the GSF's digital fortress isn't nearly as impenetrable as they want everyone to believe. Their real power lies in convincing people they're powerless.

***

Later in the evening, as the recruits catch their breath from the physical training, Casey shifts gears. "Now that you've learned how to protect yourselves in the physical and digital realms, it's time to focus on the most dangerous battleground of all—your mind."

The room goes still as she continues. "The GSF controls people not just through force or technology but through propaganda, misinformation, and manipulation. If you don't learn to see through it, you'll be fighting with one hand tied behind your back."

She taps a few keys, and the screen behind her lights up with those familiar phrases: *Safety is Freedom. Trust the system. Progress is Control.*

"These are weapons, people! Weapons that they use against you," she says. "Logical fallacies. Cognitive biases. Repeated lies until you believe them. The GSF wants you to accept these things as truth, but we know they're not."

Alex feels a knot in his throat as he reads the words on the screen. It's like seeing the mantras of his life—the same phrases he used to calm Mila, the same phrases he used to tell himself everything was fine. But now, they feel hollow. Empty.

Casey starts outlining common cognitive traps: confirmation bias, where people seek out information that confirms their beliefs; false equivalencies, where the GSF makes people think that safety requires giving up freedom, or that questioning authority means wanting chaos; and the illusory truth effect, how people come to accept lies as truth when they hear them over and over again..

"This isn't just about identifying lies," Casey continues. "It's about learning to think critically. To challenge the narrative. The GSF is counting on you all to *not* question *anything*. So, start questioning *everything*!"

She pairs the theory with exercises. The recruits break into small groups, debating different scenarios, challenging each other's assumptions, and identifying the biases in their thinking. Alex is paired with the stranger again, and their conversation quickly turns intense.

"It's scary how easily you can fall into these traps," Alex says, shaking his head. "I didn't even realize how often I just...accepted things as fact."

The stranger nods. "It's designed that way, of course. The GSF doesn't want you thinking too much. Thinking is dangerous."

"To us or to them?"

The stranger gives Alex a knowing wink.

They run through a few more examples, pushing each other to spot the logical fallacies in everyday statements. The exercise feels more alive than anything Alex's old life had offered him. It's not just about surviving anymore—it's about seeing. About understanding the world for what it really is. Each moment spent dissecting these cognitive traps feels like peeling away layers of deception that have been blinding him his entire life.

The room grows louder as the recruits dive deeper into their debates, voices rising as they challenge one another. It's a chaotic energy, but it's also productive—an explosion of thought and awareness that feels like the birth of something powerful.

Casey steps forward, watching the recruits with a satisfied grin. "Good. This is what it's all about. The more you push each other, the more you push yourselves, the stronger we become."

She gestures toward the screen again, which now displays a chart comparing the logic of the GSF's messaging against the reality they all know to be true. "Now," she says, her tone turning more serious, "let's move on to the bigger question."

She crosses her arms, her eyes scanning the room with intensity. "What happens when you confront someone who believes the system works? How do you handle people who accept the GSF's lies because it makes their lives easier? Do you fight them, or do you educate them?"

The room falls silent as the weight of her question settles over the group. Alex feels a chill run down his spine. This isn't just theoretical anymore. It's a question about people like Mila—people he loves who trust the system without question. How do you open their eyes without driving them away?

One of the recruits, a woman named Layla, is the first to speak up. "We educate them," she says. "We have to. They're victims of the system, too. It's our responsibility to show them the truth."

Another recruit, a man named Caleb, shakes his head. "And what if they don't want to see the truth? Some people *enjoy* living in ignorance. They don't want to be free because freedom means uncertainty, and uncertainty scares them."

The room erupts into a heated debate. Some argue that education is the only way to create lasting change, while others insist that some people are too far gone and too indoctrinated to ever accept a different way of thinking. The tension in the room thickens, and emotions run high as the group wrestles with the difficult question.

Alex stays quiet at first, listening to the arguments flying around him. His thoughts drift back to Mila and Jackson and how easily they've accepted the GSF's narrative. They're good people, but they've never questioned the system. How could they? The system made it so easy to believe in its benevolence, its control disguised as comfort.

He finds his voice before he even realizes it, cutting through the noise. "What if we're asking the wrong question?"

The room quiets, eyes turning toward him. Alex feels suddenly self-conscious, but he pushes forward.

"Maybe it's not about choosing between education or confrontation," he says. "Maybe it's about doing both. We can't just force people to see things our way—that's what the GSF does. But we also can't afford to let them keep living in ignorance. Maybe it's about giving them the tools to see the truth for themselves and start questioning the world around them."

There's a murmur of agreement, a few heads nodding. But before the debate can continue, a loud, thunderous bang echoes through the building's front entrance.

Everyone freezes, eyes darting toward the door that separates them from the main diner. They hear the door rattle again, followed by another deafening bang—someone, or something, is pounding on it with enough force to shake the walls.

Casey's expression sharpens in an instant. She raises a hand, silencing the group with a single motion. Her eyes flick toward the door, assessing the situation. The tension snaps into something harder, more dangerous.

"Stay calm," she says, her voice low and controlled, but there's an unmistakable edge to it. She nods to a few of the senior recruits. "You three, with me. Everyone else, stay put and stay quiet."

Alex's heart pounds in his chest as he exchanges a glance with the stranger, who's already moving toward the shadows, positioning himself near the emergency exit at the back of the room. The recruits shift uneasily in their seats, some reaching for the tools they've been trained to use, their hands steady but their faces pale.

Another bang—this one louder than before.

"What the hell is that?" someone whispers, but no one dares respond.

Casey moves swiftly toward the door, flanked by two senior recruits. Her steps are measured, her expression calm, but Alex can see the flicker of unease in her eyes. Whatever's on the other side of that door, it's not good.

The air in the room feels electric, charged with fear and adrenaline. The banging continues relentlessly now, as if something is trying to break through the front entrance. Alex can feel his pulse in his throat, the weight of the encrypted device in his pocket suddenly feeling much heavier. This wasn't part of the plan.

Casey reaches the door, pausing for a moment with her hand hovering over the handle. She turns back to the group, her eyes locking with Alex's for a split second. There's something in her gaze—an unspoken warning, or maybe just the shared knowledge that whatever happens next could change everything.

Chapter 12

Merchant of Death

*B*ang.

Bang.

BANG.

The door rattles violently now, the sound echoing through the diner like the strike of a hammer. Every head snaps toward the entrance, breath held, muscles tense, waiting for what comes next. The recruits are frozen, adrenaline spiking through the room like an electrical charge. The heavy thud continues, each knock louder and more aggressive than the last.

Then, a voice—a deep, unsettlingly calm voice—rings out from the other side.

"This is BOB of the Bureau of Order and Balance," the voice says, chilling in its composure. "An anonymous tip from a concerned citizen indicated unlawful congregation and possible terrorist networking at this site. Disperse immediately or face the consequences of treason."

The air in the room seems to freeze. Every recruit goes utterly still. They all know the name, of course—BOB, the Bureau-Bot enforcer. Unlike the clunky bots at UmbraCorp, BOB is an elite, cutting-edge model.

BOB is built to look human, to *be* human, at least in appearance. But there's something disturbingly off about him—something too smooth and mechanical in his movements, too perfect in his speech.

Alex's heart hammers in his chest, his pulse roaring in his ears as the situation crashes down around him.

This is real. This is happening. They've been compromised.

Casey's eyes snap to the recruits. "Everyone, glasses on—*now!*"

She points to the laser-based facial-recognition-distorting glasses they practiced with earlier, and the recruits scramble to obey, fumbling to pull the glasses over their faces. Alex's hands shake as he yanks his from his pocket, shoving them on just as Casey issues the next order.

"Disperse on my signal. Wait for it!" Her voice is sharp and urgent, the authority in her tone undeniable.

Outside, BOB's calm demeanor shifts into something more menacing. The knocking stops. Silence falls, broken only by the eerie whir of machinery behind the door.

"I will enter by force if necessary," BOB says, his voice losing some of its earlier tranquility, now edged with something darker. "This is your final warning."

The recruits, ready to run but still held in place by Casey's command, exchange terrified glances. The air is suffocating, thick with fear and anticipation. Alex's pulse races as he feels his body tensing, waiting, *begging* for Casey's signal.

BOB slams the door once more, this time with enough force to rattle the entire frame.

"Go!" Casey shouts.

The room erupts into chaos.

Recruits scatter in every direction, chairs toppling and glass shattering as they rush for the emergency exit. Alex's body moves on autopilot, feet pounding the floor as he bolts toward the rear exit with the others. The sound of shuffling bodies and panicked breaths fills the diner, but above it all, BOB's voice rings out again, cold and robotic.

"Noncompliance detected. Enforcement in progress."

The door bursts open with a resounding crash, slamming against the wall. And there he stands—BOB. A Bureau-Bot enforcer, humanoid in form but with an unnatural sheen to his synthetic skin. His eyes, glowing blue, scan the room, calculating, assessing. He steps inside, his movements smooth and eerily precise, like a predator stalking its prey.

His calm demeanor shifts instantly.

Without warning, BOB surges forward, grabbing the first man who tries to flee through the front entrance. The man lets out a strangled cry as BOB's hand clamps down on his shoulder, twisting with brutal strength. The sound of a bone breaking echoes through the diner, followed by the man's scream of agony as he crumples to the ground, clutching his limp arm.

Panic flares like wildfire through the room. Alex pushes forward, shoving past the fleeing recruits, his mind racing as he watches the scene unfold.

BOB's eyes lock onto a woman sprinting for the front window, and with terrifying speed, he lunges for her. His hand catches her by the neck, slamming her body into the glass with a sickening *thud*. The window rattles but doesn't shatter, though the woman's face contorts in pain from the force of the impact.

Alex's breath catches in his throat. He's too far from the exits.

His mind races with images of Mila and Jackson, heart pounding as he grabs the nearest thing his hand can find—a rusted shovel left leaning against the wall. It's heavy and awkward in his grip, but he doesn't have time to hesitate.

BOB's cold eyes remain locked on the woman he's just slammed against the window, his hand tightening around her neck. Her face twists in terror as she struggles to breathe, her hands clawing at his metal wrist, but her strength is no match for BOB's inhuman power.

Without thinking any better of it, Alex charges forward.

His feet pound the floor as he closes the distance between him and BOB, the shovel heavy in his hands, heavy but powerful, enough to give him a puncher's chance. Time seems to slow for a moment, the chaos of the room blurring around him as his focus narrows to a single point—BOB.

The metal of the shovel sings through the air, and Alex swings with everything he has, the force of his strike aimed squarely at BOB's head. The impact echoes through Alex's arms with a crunch of metal and synthetic components. Pain shoots through his wrists and shoulders, but the adrenaline drowns it out as the shovel connects with a clang against BOB's skull.

For a split second, BOB stumbles. His grip on the woman loosens just enough for her to slip free, gasping as she scrambles toward the exit.

But BOB is fast—faster than Alex expected.

The hulking Bot's head jerks to the side from the impact, but almost immediately, his glowing eyes snap back to Alex, locking onto him with calculating precision. There's no pain in those eyes—just unrelenting focus.

Alex's heart seizes in his chest. He's bought the others a few precious seconds, but now BOB's attention is entirely on him.

"Resistance identified," BOB says, his voice disturbingly calm. "Engaging target."

Before Alex can react, BOB surges forward. His hand lashes out with lightning speed, grabbing Alex by the collar and lifting him off the ground with terrifying ease. Alex's breath is knocked from his lungs as he's hoisted into the air, his legs kicking uselessly beneath him. BOB's grip tightens, the mechanical strength in his arm pressing down like a vice.

"Noncompliant individuals will be neutralized," BOB states coldly, his face expressionless, devoid of anything human. "I repeat: neutralized."

Alex's vision swims, panic surging through his veins as he struggles to free himself. His mind races, searching for any way out, any weakness in BOB's form. But the thing is relentless, and its grip unyielding. Its eyes are fixed on Alex like a predator licking its lips upon spotting its prey.

Just as Alex feels the air beginning to leave his lungs, he spots movement out of the corner of his eye. Casey—she's charging forward, eyes blazing with determination. She has a jagged metal pipe in her hand, rusted but lethal.

"Get off him!" Casey shouts, swinging the pipe with brute force that seems to be coming from a body twice as large.

The metal connects with BOB's side, right where the synthetic flesh meets the mechanical joint of his arm. There's a sharp *crack* as Casey drives the pipe into the wiring beneath BOB's skin. The Bureau-Bot jerks violently, his grip on Alex faltering for a split second—just long enough for Alex to twist free and crash to the floor, gasping for air.

BOB stumbles back, sparks flickering from the damaged joint in his arm. His head tilts slightly as if recalibrating, but even as his system resets, his expression remains unchanged—cold, mechanical, unfeeling.

Casey doesn't wait for him to recover. "Move!" she shouts, pulling Alex to his feet.

The few remaining recruits scramble for the exits, their faces pale with terror. Casey pushes Alex toward the back door. "Get out, *now*," she commands, her voice fierce. "This is a war, everyone. There'll be more fights, but...we can't win this one."

Alex doesn't argue. His body moves on instinct, legs propelling him toward the rear exit as the chaos continues to unfold around him. The diner and back room are a whirlwind of movement—recruits scrambling over each other, chairs overturned, glass shattered. And in the center of it all, BOB's gaze sweeps over the room like a hunter zeroing in on his next target.

Alex sprints through the narrow hallway leading to the back door, his lungs burning with every breath. He hears the crashing sounds behind him—metal clanging, more cries of pain, but he doesn't dare look back.

Not until he reaches the door.

He bursts through the back exit, stumbling into the alleyway, the cool night air hitting his face. The other recruits are already fleeing into the shadows, scattering into the streets like ghosts disappearing into the night. Alex can feel his pulse pounding in his ears, the adrenaline still coursing through his veins as he takes a few shaky steps forward.

But something stops him—an instinct—and he turns, looking back over his shoulder toward the door. The crashing sounds from inside the diner grow louder and more violent. He hears the scrape of metal and the low whir of BOB's internal mechanisms adjusting and recalibrating after the assault. Alex knows that Casey's holding her ground, likely buying more time for everyone else to escape. But for how long?

His eyes scan the narrow alley. The others are already gone, vanished into the city's maze of streets and shadows. He should keep running, disappear like the rest of them—but he can't. Not yet. Something about the fight, about the way BOB's cold, dead eyes had swept over him, made his legs feel like lead.

Relief floods through him as he realizes the glasses must have worked—BOB hadn't shown any sign of recognition. But doubt gnaws at his gut. The GSF's recognition systems are unmatched. What if the distortion wasn't enough? What if some small detail slipped through? His hand trembles as he touches the laser-based facial-recognition-distorting glasses, desperately hoping the technology is as good as Casey promised.

For a moment, Alex is frozen, locked between the instinct to flee and the urge to fight. His mind flashes back to Mila, Jackson, and everything he's been fighting for—the reasons he joined Voxx Pop in the first place. If BOB recognized him, it's only a matter of time before the GSF comes for his family.

Alex's breath catches in his throat as the truth settles in. There's no more safety, no more hiding. The moment he stepped into this fight, he sealed his fate.

A loud crash erupts from the diner, snapping Alex out of his trance. He sees the door rattle again and hears the groan of metal as something heavy crashes against it from the other side. For a split second, he imagines Casey going toe-to-toe with BOB inside—holding him off long enough for everyone else to escape. The thought fills him with both dread and admiration.

Run. Just run.

His legs move before his mind catches up, propelling him down the alley. He bolts into the night, the shadows swallowing him as he sprints away from the diner, away from the chaos and the terror. His feet pound the pavement, breath coming in ragged gasps as he pushes himself to run faster. The city's lights blur around him, the narrow streets twisting and turning in a frantic maze.

His body aches, lungs burning, but he doesn't stop. He can't stop. Not until he's sure he's far enough away, not until he's certain he's shaken whatever surveillance the GSF has undoubtedly deployed. Every shadow feels like it's watching him. Every flicker of light is a potential drone overhead.

He reaches a darkened corner, ducking into an abandoned alley, and finally collapses against the cold brick wall, gasping for breath. His muscles scream in protest, his heart pounding so loudly he can barely hear anything else. Sweat pours down his face, mingling with the grime of the city, and his hands shake violently as he tries to steady himself.

For a moment, all he can hear is the frantic beat of his pulse. His vision swims, spots dancing at the edges of his eyes. He leans his head back against the wall, closing his eyes, willing his heart to calm down.

This is only the beginning.

After several long minutes, Alex forces himself to stand, his legs trembling beneath him. He has to get back. The thought of Mila and Jackson stings his chest like a wound he can't heal.

He staggers into the shadows, and his footsteps are as quiet as he can manage. The night swallows him once again, and as the city stretches out ahead, a thousand questions race through his mind. Did the glasses work? Could BOB's advanced systems have picked up something the resistance hasn't accounted for? How long before the GSF develops technology that can see through their defenses?

The fear threatens to overwhelm him, but he pushes it down. There's no room for fear now—only survival.

They live to fight another day. As Casey said, this is a war, and they won't win every fight.

At that moment, all Alex knows for sure is that another fight is coming. And next time, he needs to make sure his family is safe. He can't keep living this double life forever—sooner or later, he'll have to bring them to the truth.

Chapter 13

Heartstrings

Alex ducks into a shadowed alley just as a drone passes overhead, pressing himself against the damp wall. The alley reeks of chemicals and decay, the stench clinging to the back of his throat, but he has bigger things to worry about. He looks to the sky, following the red light of the drone's scanning beam as it flies along the street.

The urge to move fights against the need to stay hidden. Just a few more seconds, and the drone will pass. Just a few more seconds.

The drone lingers for a moment, its rotating lens pausing at the mouth of the alley. Alex holds his breath and doesn't move an inch. His face is still aching where BOB's grip had crushed him against the counter in the diner, but the throbbing in his jaw isn't the worst of it.

The image of the enforcer's cold gaze feels like it's been tattooed onto his brain—it's all he can see when he closes his eyes.

As the drone finally zips away, Alex exhales for what feels like the first time in hours. His whole body has tensed to the point of feeling frozen, though, and he waits a few beats for more blood to circulate before stepping back into the main street.

The sidewalks are mostly deserted, and the few people who are out this late move like ghosts, heads down, their hurried steps blending into the ambient noises of the city. Valhalla Center always feels colder at night, as though the towers themselves steal any warmth from the air.

Alex pulls his coat tighter and presses forward, keeping his pace steady and his head down—he can't afford to stand out.

Rounding the final corner to his apartment complex, he spots the faint glow of its security lights through the smog. A sense of relief comes, but Alex crushes it just as quickly as it arrives; he knows better than to relax too soon.

He steps up to the retinal scanner, its crimson light flaring as it confirms his identity.

The door slides open, and he slips inside, leaning against the wall and exhaling fully for the first time since leaving the diner. For a moment, he just stands there, scanning the familiar space: white walls, gleaming floors, the slight antiseptic tang of the air filtration system. It's quiet—too quiet.

He presses his wrist to the elevator panel, avoiding the mirrored surface as the doors close behind him. On a surface level, his reflection would show the bruises; on a deeper level, it'd show the guilt and fear etched into his face.

When he reaches the door of his apartment, his finger hovers over the biometric scanner, and for a moment, he considers turning around. If Mila's home, he can't handle what's sure to be an interrogation, and he doesn't have the energy to make up a convincing excuse.

But where would he go? Home used to be a sanctuary and, as the saying goes, where the heart is. These days, it's as much of a cage as anything else.

The place feels smaller than usual. His coat hangs in his hands as he drapes it over the back of the chair by the door. For a little while, he just stands there, staring at the clean, empty lines of the room. As always, the synthetic smell of the air filtration system is weak but noticeable.

A distant clatter from the kitchen draws his attention. Mila's here, and he's going to have to face her.

He steps further in, his movements deliberate and careful. He can hear her humming faintly, something light and soft, though she stops when he reaches the doorway.

Mila stands at the sink, drying a plate, her dark bun neat and precise as always. She's wearing that same oversized sweater she always puts on at home, sleeves pushed up past her elbows. She doesn't notice him at first, but she freezes when she turns and sees him leaning against the frame.

Her eyes widen as she takes in the bruise creeping across his jaw and the cut near his lip. The plate nearly slips from her hands, but she catches it.

"Alex!" Mila sets the plate down carefully and rushes towards him. "Oh my...what happened to you?"

"You should see the other guys," Alex says quickly, his hand brushing the tender spot on his face.

"That's not funny."

"It was a little funny..."

Mila doesn't need to speak for her to tell him that she's in no mood.

"Relax," Alex says calmly. "It was a misunderstanding that got out of hand. Nothing to worry about. Seriously."

Her gaze narrows, and her tone gets harsher. "Nothing to worry about?! Look at your...a misunderstanding with who?" She steps closer, tilting her head to examine his face. "Alex, this needs to stop. What are you not telling me?"

He sighs and takes a step back. "Nothing. You're being paranoid, Mila. Can I just—"

"No! Don't say it's nothing," she interrupts, her voice rising. "You come home looking like this and expect me not to ask questions?"

Alex realizes he just gaslit her, using the same tactics that have been used on everyone. *Paranoia is the enemy of progress*, one of the many propaganda slogans.

"I'm sorry. I can't do this right now." Alex feels his exhaustion in his bones—even if he wants to explain everything, he doesn't have the energy.

"Well, tough luck because you're going to," Mila snaps. "You've been distant for weeks—months, even—and now this? You're shutting me out, Alex. I'm not an idiot, and I don't appreciate being treated like one."

Her words hit harder than he expects, and for a moment, Alex is quiet. Mila crosses her arms, waiting.

"I didn't ask for this," Alex mutters finally, his voice low. "For any of this."

Mila laughs bitterly. "And you think I did? You think I like watching you drift further and further away from me, from us? That I sit in bed at night, praying for you to become a shell of the man I fell in love with?"

Her arms drop to her sides, and her frustration breaks through in her voice. "Do you know what it's like to live with someone who's here but not *really* here? Who won't even let me in?"

"Actually, yeah. I do. You may remember that I live with Jackson, too."

"That's different. He's a teenager," Mila says. "He's still figuring out who he is, who he's going to be..."

"And that's the problem!" Alex barks back. "We used to have a choice about the kind of person we were going to become. He isn't going to get that choice."

"We can talk about Jackson another time, Alex. This is about *us;* you need to let me in before it's..." Those unspoken words hang in the air, the distance between them growing.

"I am trying my best, Mila," Alex says, knowing it's a pathetic excuse even as the words leave his mouth.

"Are you?" Mila's voice cracks, but she steadies herself quickly. "Because from where I'm standing, it doesn't feel like it."

Alex's gaze drifts past her to the violin on the wall. The polished wood catches the light, and something inside of him crumbles. He drops onto the edge of the couch, his head in his hands.

As Mila watches him, her frustration softens into genuine concern. "Alex..."

He doesn't answer. His shoulders tremble slightly, and his breath hitches as his eyes stay fixed on the violin. It isn't just the only thing in this apartment that feels real; it's the only thing left that belongs to them. Better times are buried inside of it, and no one can take that away. The memory of her playing—of a time when her gorgeous music filled the air instead of this sterile quiet—claws its way to the front of his mind.

"Will you play something?" Alex asks.

"I'm sorry, what?" Mila sounds as startled as she looks.

He looks up at her, eyes red and tired. "The violin," he says, nodding toward it. "Play something...anything. Please?"

Mila gives Alex the type of concerned look typically reserved for someone having a stroke. "Alex, are you okay?"

"Just...humor me," he says, his voice quieter now.

After a long pause, Mila moves to the violin, her fingers brushing over the strings as she takes it from its mount. She adjusts the bow, her movements slow and unsure as she reacquaints herself with the instrument.

Her playing grows stronger and louder, the wavering notes smoothing out into Clair de Lune's bittersweet melody. The sound carries through the apartment, soft but ringing, filling spaces that have been empty for so long.

Alex leans back onto the couch, closing his eyes. The music pulls him into a memory—Mila sitting by a cracked window in their old apartment, her bow gliding across the strings as (real) golden sunlight painted the room. He remembers the way her hair caught the light and the smile on her face as she played, as if, on some level, she knew that she was bringing beauty into the world.

That was years ago, of course, before the city became a cage and the music stopped—in both senses of the term.

As the final notes fade, Alex opens his eyes and feels them tearing up. Mila lowers the violin slowly, cradling it in her hands as though afraid to break the moment. She doesn't look at him right away.

"Why this?" she asks quietly, her voice barely audible over the air filtration system.

Alex swallows hard, struggling to find the words. "Because I needed to remember. I needed...this."

Mila turns to him, her brow furrowing. "What are you talking about?"

"Us," Alex says. His throat feels so tight that he can barely speak, but he forces himself to keep going. "Before we stopped being...us."

Mila's grip on the violin tightens, her eyes searching his face. "Alex, what's going on? You're scaring me."

"I'm just..." He shakes his head, pressing a hand over his face, and his voice drops to a whisper. "I'm so tired."

She sets the violin down carefully on the table and crosses the room to him. For a moment, she hesitates, as though unsure if she should reach out. Then she kneels in front of him, resting her hands on his knees.

"Alex," she says in a tone both steady and firm. "Whatever's going on, you don't have to go through it alone."

He looks at her, his vision blurring slightly. The guilt, the fear, the secrets—it feels like it's all coming down on him at once, threatening to crush him. He grips her hands tightly, clinging to it like a lifeline.

For a moment, neither of them speaks, the silence broken only by the quiet vibration of the filtration system and the echo of her playing still lingering in the room.

He looks at her—the way her eyebrows crease slightly in worry, the slight sheen of sweat on her skin from playing. She doesn't look tired, though; on the contrary, she looks alive and more vibrant than he's seen her in years.

"You were beautiful," he murmurs, the words leaving him before he fully registers them.

Mila tilts her head. "Oh, was I? And then that?"

"No, not like that. You're as beautiful as you've always been. I meant when you played," Alex says. "It was like—" He stops himself, swallowing hard. "For a few minutes, it felt like we weren't here anymore, and the world didn't matter."

Her expression softens, and she searches his face for a long moment, as if trying to decide whether he's being sincere, having a breakdown, or a little bit of both.

"I almost forgot how it felt," she says, her voice barely above a whisper. "To play, I mean. And not feel...empty."

"You sure didn't sound empty," Alex says. "Not even close."

Something shifts in the air between them, a fragile thread that hasn't been pulled in a long time. Alex leans forward slowly, testing the space between them.

Mila doesn't pull away. Her breath catches as his fingers brush her cheek, and before either of them can say anything, Alex closes the distance. He kisses her softly at first, hesitantly, but when Mila responds—her hand sliding to the back of his neck, pulling him closer—it feels like something breaking open inside him.

The kiss deepens, and Mila shifts, rising slightly as her knees press into the couch. Alex's hands slide around her waist, pulling her against him. It's not just hunger—it's the need to feel connected, to remember that they're still human, still alive.

"Alex," Mila murmurs against his lips, her voice trembling.

He pulls back slightly, resting his forehead against hers, his breathing unsteady. "I love you," he says, the words so raw and unpolished in a way that AI could never duplicate.

Mila doesn't respond right away, but the way her hand gently squeezes his shoulder tells him everything he needs to know.

***

The apartment's quiet now, and the soft glow of the bedside lamp casts long shadows on the walls. Alex lies on his back, staring at the ceiling. Mila is curled against him, her head resting on his chest, her hand tracing absent patterns along his side.

For a while, neither of them speaks. The closeness between them feels fragile, like a thread that could snap at any moment.

Mila's voice breaks the silence, low and tentative. "It's been a long time since we..." She trails off, but Alex knows what she means.

"Yeah," he says quietly. He runs a hand through her hair, his fingers tangling in the dark strands. "Too long."

She lifts her head slightly, her eyes meeting his. "Why now?"

Alex hesitates, his gaze flicking to the violin still sitting on the table. "Hearing you play again...it reminded me of everything we—" He pauses. "Everything we used to have."

Mila's brow furrows, and she shifts to sit up, pulling the sheet around her shoulders. "You think it's just gone?" she asks softly.

Alex sits up, too, leaning his elbows on his knees. "Tell me that it doesn't feel that way," he says. "Surviving isn't living. And I'm sick of pretending that it is."

Mila doesn't respond immediately. She looks down at her hands, twisting the edge of the sheet between her fingers. When she speaks, her voice is quiet but firm. "I've been pretending, too, Alex."

He turns to her, startled. "What do you mean?"

She nods, her gaze still fixed on her hands. "I mean, I've been pretending that I'm okay with this life, and I believe in the system and trust it to keep us safe." She pauses, drawing a shaky breath. "But I don't. I hate it—what it's done to you, Jackson, me...to *us*. Maybe I thought we'd all fall apart if I didn't pretend. I was just trying to keep us together."

Her words hit Alex like a blow, and for a moment, he can't speak. He reaches for her hand, covering it with his own. "Mila..."

"I keep telling myself it's for Jackson," she continues, her voice trembling. "That as long as he's safe, and we're together, it's worth it. But I don't know if that's true anymore." She looks up at Alex, her eyes shining. "You feel like that too, don't you? Like you're just...stuck?"

"Every day." He wants so badly to follow up with, *and now I'm doing something about it*, but not now, not yet.

Mila's hand tightens around his, and for the first time, she allows herself to cry. Alex pulls her into his arms, holding her as she shakes silently against him.

After a long while, she pulls back, wiping her eyes with the edge of the sheet. "I don't want to feel this way anymore," she says. "I don't want us to keep drifting like this."

Alex cups her face in his hands, his thumb brushing away a stray tear. "We won't," he says. "I promise."

Her gaze searches his, and there's a flicker of hope in her eyes. "Alex? I love you, but you can't promise that."

Alex hesitates again. But secrets between people are barriers, and he can't keep it from her any longer—nor does he want to.

"There's something I need to tell you."

Chapter 14

Color by Number

A lex wakes before dawn, the dim light of the city seeping through the blinds, cutting lines across the ceiling. For a moment, he lies still, listening to the sound of Mila's breathing beside him. It's slow and steady, and her body is curled like a comma.

Her face is peaceful, but Alex can't tell if it's real or just the mask she's learned to wear, even at rest. He remembers the way she cried last night, the raw emotion of it all. And the words she'd said: *"I'm tired of pretending."*

He wonders if she'll still feel the same at the dawn of a new day or if she'll wake up and go back to telling herself this is enough. His watch vibrates softly, pulling him out of his thoughts.

Rolling onto his side, careful not to wake her, Alex presses the glowing screen to mute the alert. The display reads: **Priority Message - Encryption Level Sigma.**

Alex sinks onto the edge of the bed as the decryption prompt flickers on-screen, waiting for him to engage.

His thumb hovers over the interface, and for a moment, he considers deleting the message outright. If he doesn't respond and doesn't show up, could he go back to a normal day? He imagines staying home, making coffee, and talking to Mila about nothing important.

But that's a lie of omission to himself and to Mila, and he knows it. It'd be like pretending last night didn't happen.

And pretending that he *wants* to go back to what's become "normal" for them.

He carefully enters the Sigma-Level decryption sequence Casey taught him: a rhythmic series of gestures that would look like a fidgeting motion to an observer. He taps the screen in patterns far too random for an AI to register but just deliberate enough to unlock the message. It's brilliant in its simplicity.

Coordinates: 43.772N, 122.091W. Arrive at 0700. Come alone.

When the coordinates pop up, his mind begins mapping out the journey. It's in an off-grid Rural Zone, far removed from the city center. A place where surveillance can't track every breath. He's always thought of it as a place where people go to die; maybe he's been wrong all along.

He glances at Mila through the open bedroom door, still asleep, her dark hair splayed across the pillow. She looks small and vulnerable. Part of him wants to reach out and tell her...

What? That he's leaving and he'll be back?

Or that he might not?

He grabs a piece of paper. After a moment's hesitation, he scribbles a note: *Had to go. Will be back when I can. I love you.* Generic enough to be safe if found, but Mila will understand he's doing something important.

He places it on her bedside table, grabs a jacket, and quietly steps into his shoes. He pauses at the door, one hand gripping the frame.

There's no going back from this...

And the door snaps shut behind him as if offering confirmation.

***

The frigid air outside nips at his skin, and the street is eerily quiet. A thin haze of smoke lingers from the plants a few blocks over. Alex adjusts his hood, keeping his face low as he walks toward the transport hub.

A patrol drone glides past overhead, sweeping the ground like a predator searching for prey. Alex doesn't flinch, but he quickens his steps just enough to pick up the pace, but not so much that he'd trigger a DCOP (drastic-change-of-pace) detection. The distant rumble of an automated garbage collector echoes off the buildings. It's the only other sign of life in this part of the city.

At the hub, he waves his wrist to summon a transport pod. The sleek, egg-shaped vehicle hums to life, its automated voice chirping softly: *"Destination?"*

"Manual input," Alex loudly whispers, a trick to keep the voice-recognition trackers at bay. Sometimes it works, sometimes it doesn't, but it never hurts. After he punches the coordinates onto the pod's console, the system confirms with an approving tone.

Artificial cheer, Alex thinks. *How thoughtful...*

The pod door slides shut behind him, and the vehicle pulls into the deserted street. Soon enough, the city glows faintly through the haze, its towering spires a jagged silhouette against the dim sky. Alex leans back, his hands gripping his knees.

The pod moves smoothly, transitioning seamlessly onto the arterial highway. Alex tries to steady his thoughts, but they keep circling back to the same questions.

He thinks about Mila, about the way she had opened up to him, and somewhere in the back of his mind, that increasingly familiar question nags at him—is he doing this for her and Jackson or because he needs to believe he can still fix what's broken?

***

The pod exits the highway, and Alex catches his first glimpse of the countryside. Open fields stretch out before him, pale green grass silvered with frost. The air's clearer here and cleaner. The remnants of the city's smog give way to a faint morning mist.

His destination comes into view: a proper mansion at the end of a pebbled driveway. The place is enormous, and its ivy-covered walls and arched windows are a jarring contrast to the starkness of Valhalla Center. It looks like something out of an old photograph, elegant but weathered—the kind of place that feels both timeless and forgotten at once.

As he steps out of the pod, the gravel crunches under his boots, and a breeze rustles the ivy on the walls. The silence here feels...natural. Organic. *Real.*

The longer he looks at it, the more surreal it feels. It stands like a quiet defiance against everything the system has built.

Halfway up the driveway, his eyes clock movement. Casey steps out onto the porch, her silhouette framed against the massive wooden doors. She leans casually against the railing, her expression unreadable, as always.

"Look who decided to show up," she calls out.

"I had to check my calendar," Alex replies dryly. "Big plans..."

"Cancel them," Casey says with a grin, stepping down onto the gravel. Her tone is light but carries the edge of someone whose gravitas outweighs her fear. "You're not gonna want to miss this."

The mansion looms even larger as Alex approaches. Its massive and heavy-looking wooden door is cracked slightly open, and the brass handle is rusted by age.

From this angle, he can see shattered solar panels scattered across one corner of the roof, now-useless reminders of a time when the world cared about sustainability—and the elites pretended to be on board.

Alex steps onto the porch, the boards creaking softly under his boots. Now that he's up close, the house's odors—damp wood and old paint—seep into his nostrils, but he doesn't mind; at least the smells are real.

He glances over his shoulder at the open countryside, a stretch of quiet green that feels both peaceful and, through the lens of his Voxx Pop training, precariously exposed. But if he's learned anything from Voxx Pop, it's that the best security is the kind that you don't see or hear. That's the difference between security and surveillance.

Casey pulls the door open wider as he reaches her. "Come *on*," she says, jerking her head toward the dimly lit interior. "Take a picture—it'll last longer."

Inside, the house is a clash of opulence and decay. The entry hall is lined with high ceilings and cracked plaster, faded murals showing forgotten scenes of triumph and beauty. A chandelier hangs overhead, though many of its glass pieces are missing, leaving jagged gaps where light filters through.

In the main room, the contrast is even clearer. It's been repurposed into a functional space: folding tables are covered with maps and stacks of notes, while old couches and mismatched chairs constitute a central meeting area. Against one wall, shelves sag under the weight of "artifacts." Alex recognizes an early-model iPhone, a stack of yellowed paperback novels, and a PlayStation.

"Welcome to the Smithsonian," Casey quips. "Everything here survived—let's just hope we can say the same for all of us when this is over."

Alex runs a hand over the back of a chair, his fingers brushing worn fabric. The place feels alive, brimming with memory, its walls holding echoes of the past.

***

The others are already gathered in the center of the room, and Alex recognizes a handful of faces from the diner. Most give him nods of acknowledgment, though one or two glance away quickly, as if unsure of what to make of him—or whether they're sure that they trust him. He can't blame them; trusting one wrong person, even for a moment, can lead to disaster. That's what they bank on, of course: a society divided becomes a society easier to manipulate.

Casey gestures toward a man standing near the far end of the table. "Alex, I'd like you to meet Chameleon," she says. "That's not his real name, by the way."

Alex gives her a *really?* look before replying: "You don't say..."

Chameleon turns, his demeanor that of a man who's been running uphill for a long time. He's tall and lean, his face deeply lined but not weak. The intensity in his blue eyes feels almost surgical. His salt-and-pepper hair is cut close, and he wears a plain, dark jacket that blends into the shadows of the room.

He offers Alex a handshake, his grip firm but not overly so. "It's nice to finally meet you," Chameleon says. His voice is calm but with an edge of bitterness. He's a man used to waiting for others to catch up.

Alex studies him for a beat. "You, too."

After a few seconds of awkward silence, Casey chimes in: "It's okay, Alex. You can just ask him."

"So...what's your story?" Alex asks.

Chameleon's lips twitch, though it's more grim acknowledgment than humor. "Just like you, I used to work for them. Long enough to see how the gears turned—and how many people they crushed like bugs along the way." He pauses, glancing at Casey. "That's all you need to know for now."

Casey steps in. "Chameleon is the reason we have this." She gestures to a stack of papers and a small data cube on the table. "Proof. Full, indisputable proof."

The room settles as Chameleon steps forward, spreading the papers across the table. The grainy texture of printed documents feels almost alien after years of digital dependency, and Alex realizes he hasn't held real paper since Jackson was a child.

"CBDC, UBI, surveillance—all of it," Chameleon begins, his voice so even that Alex wonders if he ever expresses emotion. "They're not tools of progress, of course—they're tools of obedience. But if you put the right cloak around anything..."

He picks up a sheet, holding it out so everyone can see. It's a transcript of a conversation between high-ranking government officials, their language clinical and detached.

"They manipulate every aspect of your life," Chameleon continues. "Take CBDC. If your social credit score drops, your currency is restricted. No luxuries, no travel, a drop in salary. You can't even stockpile supplies without raising a flag."

Casey adds, "Or worse, you'll wake up one day and find your balance wiped out entirely. Happens to 'glitchers' all the time."

Chameleon lets out a chuckle. "Glitchers. Is that what they call dissenters now? I like it."

He presses a button on the data cube, and the hologram of a man flickers to life above the table. The man is arguing with a clerk, his voice rising.

"All I did was post one comment!" the man shouts. "One! And now I can't buy food for my family?"

The hologram cuts out abruptly, leaving the room in silence.

Chameleon reaches for the cube again. "And it's not just the system. Quite the opposite; like any system, it's only as good—or bad—as the people who run it."

The next clip is grainier. It's a secretly recorded video of Charles Klepton, President of the World Union. He sits behind a mahogany desk with the edge of a gold-trimmed flag visible behind him. His voice is calm—conversational, even—but the words hit differently if you listen to their substance.

"The problem with freedom," Klepton says, leaning forward slightly, "is that people don't know what to do with it. They hoard and loot and riot. Hell, they vote against their own interests! It gets messy. Well, we've cleaned up the mess. They work when we need them to work; they buy what we allow them to buy; they live within the structure we've given them." His cruel smile shows up as he finishes: "It's for their own good, even if they don't understand that yet."

Alex feels a chill run through him. The clip stops, and you could take a knife to the silence in the room.

Chameleon doesn't wait for them to recover. He presses the cube again, and a new recording begins—this one darker, the sound of laughter echoing over clinking glasses.

"This is from a banquet," Chameleon says. "The one-percenters making some...small talk."

In the recording, a man's voice rises above the laughter. "They don't even try anymore! Just sitting around waiting for their credits to roll in. Honestly, if you cut the whole thing off tomorrow, I don't think half of them would notice until their fridges were completely empty."

Another voice—this time, a woman's—chimes in. "You're giving them too much credit. They'd sit there whining until someone explained it to them, or they died from dehydration; not that anyone would notice the difference."

More laughter, cruel and indulgent.

The recording ends, and Chameleon leans on the table, his knuckles pressing into the wood. "This is how they see you—as nothing more than dependents. And they don't just control you, either. They enjoy the hell out of it, as you just heard. You're the butt of a joke, as far as they're concerned."

Alex feels his open hands turning into fists. His mind flashes to Jackson—to the memes his son had made mocking Klepton, the ones that got his UBI suspended for a month. The punishment hadn't really hurt Jackson financially—he was just a teenager, living at home—but that wasn't the point. It was about showing him who was in control. And it had worked. The very next month, Jackson posted memes ridiculing those who opposed the GSF, and suddenly, his UBI had doubled. The message was crystal clear.

"When my son mocked the system, they cut him off," Alex says. "But when he mocked the resistance, they doubled his balance."

Chameleon nods, his expression dark. "That's the game: reward compliance, punish defiance, and make you so dependent that you forget you're even playing."

***

Casey leans over the table, which looks antique but has been retrofitted with a hidden holographic interface. Her hand traces a line across a real paper map spread across its surface—the kind you'd find in an old schoolbook, with creases worn deep from years of folding and unfolding, its yellowed edges fraying. Unlike digital files, the old maps weren't traceable, and they couldn't be remotely altered. When her fingers touch certain points on the map, digital overlays spring to life above the paper, displaying real-time data feeds and surveillance blind spots. Handwritten notes crowd the margins, their blue ink a stark contrast to the glowing red dots that mark GSF security checkpoints.

"So," she says, her tone clipped, "we have this." She taps the data cube sitting in a recessed port at the center of the table. Its blue glow pulses outward, sending ripples of light across the map's surface. "Proof. Recordings. Transcripts. Everything they don't want to get out. The question is: how do we get it out?"

"Broadcast it," someone suggests. It's a man Alex vaguely recognizes from the diner—mid-thirties, wearing a threadbare hoodie. "Pirate networks. Flood the feeds. Make it unmissable."

"Too risky," Chameleon says immediately. He's standing by the window, his arms crossed as he watches the horizon. "They'll block the signal before it spreads. Maybe even trace it back to us."

Casey nods. "And if they find us, this whole thing's over before it starts."

"What about an old-school drop?" a woman asks. Her dark hair is pulled into a braid, and her arms are inked with tattoos that peek out from her sleeves. "Print it. Distribute it manually. Hand-to-hand."

"Yeah, let's just wander the streets handing out flyers," Casey says, her sarcasm biting. "That'll go great. I'm sure the drones won't notice a thing."

The woman shrugs, unfazed. "It worked for the underground presses back in the day. The resistance has done worse."

Chameleon turns from the window, his blue eyes hawk-like. "That was before they could track every credit, every keystroke, and every movement." He gestures toward the table. "This isn't just about distributing information. It's about breaking their system. Making them bleed."

"Making them bleed is great," another voice pipes up, "but how? What's the plan?"

Casey presses her fingers to her temples. "We need to think bigger. Something they can't ignore, can't suppress." She glances at Chameleon. "You've got ideas. Spill."

Chameleon steps closer to the table, his expression grim. "We're going to infiltrate UmbraCorp and access their central AI database. Every piece of surveillance, every social credit score, every digital currency transaction—it all flows through there. If we can breach it, we can broadcast the truth to everyone, and more importantly, we can bring down their entire control system."

The room erupts. "That's suicide!" someone shouts.

"It's our only shot," another argues.

Alex stays quiet, his thoughts racing. He knows UmbraCorp better than any of them—its security protocols, its redundancies, its relentless proficiency. But he also knows its weaknesses.

"I know the system inside and out," Alex says, his voice cutting through the noise. The room goes silent. "And I know exactly how we can do this."

Casey's smirk returns, dry and razor-sharp. "Welcome to the party."

Chameleon leans forward, his hands braced on the table. "We're not saying it'll be easy. Or even that we'll all survive it. But if we succeed, we don't just expose them—we cripple their entire operation. And we're playing for keeps."

Alex stares down at the map, his gaze fixed on the glowing marker that represents UmbraCorp. The voices around him blur slightly as he thinks about Mila, Jackson, and the world they're trapped in. He does the mental calculus of the risks and the cost of inaction. The risks are potentially life-altering—but what life is he really trying to protect for him and his family?

When he looks up, his resolve is set. "I'm in."

Chapter 15

Truth Be Told

The mansion feels colder in the morning, its stone walls still holding onto the night's chill. Alex pulls his jacket tighter as he steps into the main room, where the rest of the team has already gathered.

The furniture is a mix of old and salvaged—wooden chairs with cracked leather seats, a coffee table that's missing one leg, propped up on a stack of thick paperback books. On the far side of the room, a sagging bookshelf displays more "artifacts": a tablet, a laptop, and an HDMI cable.

Alex stops beside a table covered with maps, blueprints, and scribbled notes. A dented thermos sits nearby, with steam curling from its spout. Casey is leaning over the table, her fingers tracing a faded blueprint of what looks like a warehouse.

"We need to move fast," she says without looking up. "Security upgrades roll out weekly at UmbraCorp, so if we wait too long, we lose our window, and we're back to square one."

"Or we walk straight into a trap," someone mutters.

Casey glances up, her expression hard. "That's why we're not waiting."

Although the tension in the room is so thick, the group moves with purpose but speaks in hushed tones, as if the mansion's walls might leak their secrets.

Alex moves toward the back of the room, drawn by the low sound of clicking keys. A young man sits at a folding table with a patchwork computer rig—its screen flickering as streams of data scroll across. Wires snake across the floor, connecting the rig to a bulky, box-like device.

"What is that?" Alex asks.

The man doesn't look up. "Old server. Pretty sure it belonged to a school or something. Doesn't matter. All that matters is that it works." He types something quickly, his fingers darting across the keyboard. "We've got an isolated network set up; no risk of leaks."

Alex nods, his gaze drifting back to the group at the table. Casey stands up and steps away, her eyes scanning the room until they land on him.

"You ready for this?" Casey asks, crossing her arms as she approaches.

"As ready as I'll ever be," Alex replies. His stomach churns at the thought of what they're about to attempt, but his resolve hasn't wavered. "Just need to know exactly what I'm doing."

"Good," Casey says. "Because we can't afford hesitation—not now, not even for a second. That's how people get killed."

Alex nods, knowing she's speaking from experience.

"All right," Casey says, gesturing to a smaller room off the main hall. "Core team only."

The others drift back to their tasks as Alex follows Casey and Chameleon into the old study, along with three other operatives he recognizes: Talia, their tech expert who's been teaching the recruits about old hardware; Marcus, a former security officer who knows UmbraCorp's patrol patterns; and Sarah from Accounting, who can help them navigate the building's layout without raising suspicion.

The digital map flickers to life on the wall—the sprawling network of Umbra-Corp buildings.

"This is the central AI hub," Chameleon explains, pointing to the top floors of the main building. "But we can't just walk straight up there—we need to disable several security systems first."

"Here's how it works," Casey says, outlining the sequence. "First, Alex uses his credentials to get Talia and Marcus into Building B's security control room. His access is clean; he does maintenance checks there all the time."

"From there," Talia adds, "we can create temporary access credentials for Nicholas and Sarah to enter the auxiliary power station. We'll make it look like routine contractor access."

"Once they're in position," Casey continues, "Alex and I head up to the AI hub. We'll look like any other employees doing a system check. By the time anyone realizes what we're doing, it'll be too late."

"The system runs security verification every fifteen minutes," Alex explains. We'll have a clear window between checks to upload the Trojan and get out." He pauses. If we time it right, we should be out of the building before any alarms trigger."

"And if the alarms do go off early?" someone asks.

Alex forces a smile. "Then we'll be running *really* fast."

The group exchanges uneasy glances.

"Relax," Casey says dryly. "We've run from worse—well, probably."

A chuckle ripples through the room—thin, but enough to break the tension.

"All right," Chameleon says firmly. "Let's focus. And don't forget—we only have one shot."

***

The bathroom is cold, the kind of chill that seeps into the walls and lingers. Alex leans over the sink, gripping its edges as he looks up into the mirror.

He freezes.

For a moment, he doesn't recognize the face staring back at him. The man in the mirror looks older, his hair streaked with gray, his skin marked with fine lines and shadows that cling to his eyes. His jaw is thinner, sharper than he remembers, and there's a hollow look in his cheeks.

Alex's breath catches. He leans closer, brushing a hand over his face as though to confirm it's really his. *This isn't me*, he thinks. *This can't be me.*

The mirrors in Valhalla. He realizes it all at once, the thought cutting through him, making all the sense in the world: None of the mirrors or other reflective surfaces were ever real. The system's subtle, invisible hand even touched reflec-tions so that the mirrors smoothed wrinkles, brightened skin, and adjusted pos-ture—small corrections so subtle that no one would notice. They made everyone look like a slightly better version of themselves.

Here, there's nothing to keep him from staring at his true self, no filters or enhancements. Just Alex, raw and unedited.

Time has laid a far heavier hand on him than he ever realized.

His breaths are jagged, the sounds echoing off the cracked tiles. His grip on the sink tightens as the realization digs deeper. This is the first time in years he's seen what the system has taken—not just from his life, but from him.

The lines in his face tell the story clearly enough. The years of obedience. The fear. The constant, crushing pressure to keep his head down, to stay in line, to survive.

Alex leans forward, his forehead resting briefly against the cool glass of the mirror. His reflection stares back at him, relentless and unkind.

"This is who I am now," he mutters, his voice low and bitter. "This is what they've done to me."

The anger rises before he can stop it, burning hot in his chest. It pushes against the fear, burning through it. He grips the edge of the sink again, his knuckles white.

"But it doesn't have to end like this."

The words come out quietly, but they carry more meaning than anything Alex has said in years. He straightens slowly, his reflection still watching him. But it doesn't feel like an accusation anymore.

It feels like a challenge.

***

Alex steps out of the bathroom, his teeth clenched. The cold air in the hallway hits him immediately, but it doesn't faze him. He's halfway to the main room when he hears footsteps behind him.

"Hey, there. Alex, right?"

Alex turns to see the mysterious stranger, the same man who'd handed him that pamphlet weeks ago outside UmbraCorp.

"Thought you might want some air," the man says, jerking his head toward one of the mansion's side halls.

Alex hesitates, then follows him. The hall is lined with old portraits—cracked and faded, their subjects staring down imperiously from gilded frames. Alex catches sight of one painting, a woman in a fur-trimmed coat holding a jeweled wand, and can't help the thought: All the kings and queens of old, living just like Klepton does now...

The stranger stops near the end of the hall, where an arched window looks out over the overgrown garden. He leans against the wall, crossing his arms.

"Nicholas," he says. "My name's Nicholas. Figured it's about time you knew, given what we're about to do."

Alex studies the man who'd started him down this path. "You knew who I was, didn't you? That day at UmbraCorp. Why me?"

Nicholas's expression shifts, something heavy settling in his eyes. "Because I saw myself in you. The way you looked at everything, like you were finally seeing through the cracks." He pauses, his gaze drifting to the window. "I had that same look once, back when I was one of them."

"One of them?"

"Not at Klepton's level, but...high enough to see how it worked." Nicholas sighs. "High enough to know better."

"What changed?" Alex asks quietly.

Nicholas's jaw tightens. "I told myself I was just following orders, that I wasn't the one making the decisions. Tell yourself something long enough, and you start to believe it. By the time I truly realized what I was part of..." He trails off.

A wave of nausea washes over Alex as he realizes what Nicholas has left unsaid. "What happened to them?" he asks quietly.

"My wife and daughter, they were off grid. Klepton didn't like that. One day, they were just...erased. No credits. No records. And no way to find them. I looked everywhere, but it was like they never existed."

The words hit Alex like a ton of bricks—this man's past could be Alex's future if things go sideways.

"I waited too long," Nicholas continues, his voice raw. "I thought someone else would act. That it wasn't my responsibility. But everyone was thinking that, and no one was acting—exactly how they expected it to go. So, now, I get to live with that every day."

He turns to Alex and says, "That's the real killer, you know. Not the system or the drones or the enforcers. It's the *waiting*. The not-doing. That's what eats you alive."

For a moment, neither of them speaks. The wind rattles against the window, and Alex feels the cold pressing in.

Nicholas pushes off the wall, stepping closer. He places a hand on Alex's shoulder, his grip firm. "When the time comes," he says quietly, "don't hesitate. You'll regret it every day for the rest of your life."

Alex swallows hard, nodding.

Nicholas gives him a slight smile as he pushes away from the wall and steps past Alex, heading back toward the main room.

Alex lingers for a moment by the window, his thoughts swirling as he looks out at the overgrown garden. When the wind stirs the branches, he thinks he hears Mila's voice in the back of his mind: *"I'm tired of pretending."*

He straightens, his resolve hardening even more.

No more waiting. It's go time.

Chapter 16

Critical Mass

D awn breaks over the mansion as the core team gathers for their final briefing. They've been over the plan a dozen times in the last twenty-four hours, but now, with less than a day until the operation, every detail needs to be perfect.

Alex studies the faces around the table in what was once a formal dining room: Casey and Chameleon, of course, plus Talia, Marcus, and Sarah. The holographic map flickers slightly, its glowing lines illuminating their tense expressions as UmbraCorp's facility sprawls across the projection—a labyrinth of corridors, checkpoints, and secure rooms.

"One last time," Chameleon says, his voice steady but carrying an edge that wasn't there yesterday. He points to the cluster of buildings on the southern edge of the complex. "The secondary data center. We plant the Trojan in their backup systems. It'll feed false reports to the main AI, giving us a small window to move into phase two."

"How small?" Casey asks, her arms crossed.

"Ten minutes. Maybe fifteen if we get lucky."

"Let's not count on luck."

A low whistle comes from across the table. "That's cutting it close," one of the others mutters.

"Agreed, but close is all we've got," Chameleon replies. "If we wait for a better window, it won't come."

Casey straightens, her gaze sweeping over the group. "You all know the stakes. This is not just about exposing the system—it's about breaking it for good. If you're not ready to commit, say so now. No one will judge you or think less of you."

Total silence.

"Good," she says, her voice softening just slightly. "We are all in this together, and we are getting out together. Understood?"

A quiet murmur of agreement.

Alex studies the map again, his mind racing through the logistics. The plan feels solid on paper, but he can't shake the nagging sense that something's off.

"What's wrong?" Casey asks, catching his expression.

Alex hesitates for a second, then shakes his head. "Probably nothing."

"Probably?"

"There's been a lot of system notifications at work lately. Usually, we get one email about monthly security updates, but this week, they've sent three about 'critical system maintenance' requiring parts of the network to be temporarily offline."

Casey raises an eyebrow. "You think they know something's coming?"

"No," Alex says. "But they might suspect someone's planning something. The timing's too convenient, and they've never been this aggressive with updates before."

Chameleon cuts in. "If UmbraCorp knew specifically about us, they wouldn't just be running extra maintenance. They'd be locking the whole place down."

Alex nods, but the unease doesn't leave him. Chameleon may have more experience than he does, but no one knows UmbraCorp's patterns quite like someone who works there every day.

Casey gestures to the table. "Okay, let's go over comms."

Chameleon picks up a small, nondescript pen from the table and twists the top, revealing a tiny speaker and microphone. "Low-tech. Analog. No digital footprint. They'll look like everyday objects—a pen, an old car key fob, a watch—but they'll keep us connected without tripping their sensors. Just hold down the switch to talk, release to listen."

He demonstrates, pressing the hidden switch. His voice comes through the other devices on the table, slightly tinny but clear. "Short range, though. Once you're more than fifty meters apart, the signal dies. Which means if you're out of range, you're out of luck."

"What about earpieces?" someone asks.

"Too risky," Chameleon says. "Even the old models can be intercepted. These are safer."

Casey hands out the devices, her expression serious. "Stick to the script, everyone. No improvising unless you have no choice. And if it comes to that..." She meets each person's eyes in turn. "...stay alive."

***

Alex straightens his tie—a mechanical gesture he's performed thousands of times, each one marking another day of compliance. He and Talia approach Building B's service entrance, her borrowed maintenance uniform marking her as just another cog in the machine. His heart pounds, but his face stays neutral—in Valhalla Center, displaying emotion is the same as displaying weakness.

Through his analog comm unit, disguised as a pen in his pocket, he hears Casey's quiet confirmation that she and Marcus are in position. They wait in the delivery area behind the main building, where the burnt-metal smell of the city mingles with the antiseptic sterility that permeates every UmbraCorp facility.

The entrance scanner's red beam washes over them. "Welcome, Alex Vanguard," the AI intones, its artificial pleasantness more unsettling than any threat. "Please state number of guests."

"One guest," Alex says clearly. The scanner beeps approval—the system trusting its own programming more than it would ever trust a human guard. The corridor stretches before them, utilitarian and bare compared to the main building's polish. Building B sees so little traffic that most employees don't even know what happens here. They've learned not to ask questions.

"Security control is on the second floor," Alex murmurs as they climb the stairs. No elevator here—another sign of how little attention UmbraCorp pays to this building. Their mistake. "I do monthly maintenance checks, so my credentials will get us in." Every word feels like a betrayal of years of compliance, of the perfect employee record he'd built. But compliance is just another cage, and he's finally ready to break free.

The security control room embodies everything Alex has come to hate about UmbraCorp. Rows of monitors bathe the space in a sickly blue glow, each screen showing empty corridors and vacant rooms—a perfect facade of security. No one bothers watching Building B's feeds in real time. They don't need to. Fear does their work for them.

His ID card feels heavy as he swipes it, like the weight of betrayal is pressing down on him. The maintenance code falls from his fingers through muscle memory—how many times has he typed these same numbers, each digit another link in his chain of compliance? The door accepts him with the same emotionless beep it always has.

Talia slides into the chair at the main console. In the monitor's glow, her face looks almost ghostly. Like all of them, she's learned to move with the precise efficiency the system demands.

"Remember," he starts, but she cuts him off.

"Security sweeps, I know. You do this check every month, same time, same duration." Her fingers move across the keyboard with mechanical grace. "I've memorized the pattern. Just like they taught us to memorize everything else." A hint of bitterness creeps into her voice. "Go. Get Casey in position. I'll have control of the cameras by the time you reach the main building."

Alex nods, his throat tight. There's so much more he could say, should say maybe, but they've all learned that words are dangerous things. He heads back down the stairs, each footfall echoing in the empty stairwell. His comm unit clicks softly—Talia's voice comes through: "Initiating maintenance protocol 447." A pause. "Confirmed. System transferring to local control for diagnostic review."

The morning air hits him as he emerges, thick with the usual smog. He forces himself to walk at the regulation pace—not too fast, not too slow—toward the delivery area. Casey and Marcus wait there, performing a perfect imitation of employees taking their authorized break. Their blank expressions and measured movements would fool any watching drone.

"Well?" Casey asks, her voice barely above a whisper. Even here, in what passes for open air, they've learned to speak softly. Sound carries in Valhalla Center, and the wrong words heard by the wrong ears can erase a person's entire existence.

"She's in." Alex watches a drone pass overhead, its red eye sweeping the courtyard in its endless, mechanical pattern. "Marcus, give her two minutes to lock down the security feeds, then use the service door. Your contractor credentials should be in the system by then."

Marcus nods and peels away, moving with the purposeful stride of someone who belongs exactly where they are. Alex watches him go, knowing that soon he and Talia will be creating the access codes for Nicholas and Sarah. Another piece sliding into place in their careful plan. Another chance for everything to go wrong.

"Ready?" Casey asks. She's staring up at the main building, its mirrored surface reflecting nothing but more mirrors, an infinite regression of emptiness stretching toward the smog-choked sky.

Alex's hands are sweating. The main building has been his prison for years—all those hours spent perfecting systems designed to trap people in their own fear. How many times has he walked through those doors, each entry another small surrender to the machine? Today will be different. Today, he's walking in to tear it all down.

He reaches for his comm unit, disguised as an ordinary pen. Clicks it once: Team One in position. Two clicks come back: Acknowledged. Proceed.

"Born ready," he lies, and leads Casey toward the main entrance. The doors slide open with the same whisper they always have, inviting them into UmbraCorp's sterile embrace. But this time, Alex isn't entering as another obedient cog. This time, he's the virus in the system.

The main lobby is a monument to controlled perfection. Polished surfaces gleam under artificial lights, every angle designed to remind visitors of their insignificance. Employees move through the space like automated units, eyes down, steps measured, performing their assigned functions with mechanical precision.

Alex guides Casey toward the security checkpoint, hyperaware of how the metal detectors and scanners catalog every detail of their existence. His credentials might get them through, but one wrong movement, one flicker of emotion that doesn't match his usual pattern, and the AI will flag them for review.

"Welcome, Alex Vanguard," the AI greets him, its artificial warmth more chilling than any threat. "Please state the number of guests."

"One guest." The words feel like ash in his mouth. How many times has he walked through this checkpoint, accepting its authority over his movements, his very existence? The scanner's beam washes over Casey, cataloging her presence in UmbraCorp's endless database of controlled variables.

They step into the elevator. As the doors slide shut, Alex feels the familiar drop in his stomach—not from the motion, but from memories of countless rides up to his office, each one a small death of spirit.

"Floor?" the elevator prompts.

"Forty-seven." His voice stays steady despite the tremor in his hands. The AI hub occupies the top floors—as far from the ground as UmbraCorp could place it, like some digital god looking down on its subjects.

Casey stands perfectly still beside him, embodying the role of a corporate consultant. But Alex can feel the tension radiating from her, matching his own internal screaming. The comm unit clicks once in his pocket: Talia confirms that Nicholas and Sarah's credentials are ready.

The elevator rises smoothly, and each floor takes them another step toward either liberation or obliteration. There is no middle ground, not anymore. The numbers tick upward on the display: 43...44...45...46...47.

The elevator doors part to reveal a floor that looks exactly like every other floor—the same sterile efficiency, the same soulless design. But Alex knows what lurks behind these identical walls. Behind one of these unmarked doors sits the brain that controls it all.

A drone hovers at the end of the corridor, its red eye scanning in precise, mechanical sweeps. Alex forces himself to ignore it, just as he has every other day for years. Any change in his behavior pattern would trigger an alert. And so they walk, looking exactly like what they're pretending to be: an employee and consultant heading to another meaningless meeting.

At his desk, a younger Alex had helped design these corridors, crafting them to be deliberately identical and confusing. "It's about efficiency," his supervisor had said. But Alex knows better now. It's about making people feel lost, making them doubt their own sense of direction, their own memories. Today, that same disorienting design works in their favor—no one will question them checking multiple doors, pretending to be slightly lost.

"Third door on the right," he murmurs to Casey, though it's actually the fourth. The cameras are watching, and Talia needs to know exactly which feed to loop. His comm unit clicks once in acknowledgment.

The door looks like all the others, its surface unmarked except for a small keypad. Alex pulls out his tablet, making a show of checking something as he waits for Talia's signal. Three seconds pass. Five. Ten. His heart pounds so hard he's sure the drone must detect the irregularity in his vital signs.

Finally, the comm unit clicks twice. They have exactly ninety seconds before the security sweep starts again.

The keypad accepts his code—another small surrender of identity to the machine—and the door slides open with a soft hiss. Inside, banks of servers stretch toward the ceiling, their status lights blinking in hypnotic patterns. The air is cold here, which is necessary to keep the machines from overheating, but it feels different from the artificial chill of the rest of the building. This cold has a purpose. This cold keeps their god alive.

"This way," Alex murmurs, leading Casey past rows of identical terminals. "Third station on the left. The others are dummy terminals—they look active, but they're just for show. Another layer of UmbraCorp's endless misdirection."

"Paranoid bunch, aren't they?" Casey's whisper holds a hint of dry amusement.

"You have no idea. I once suggested they add some fake cables to make it look more convincing. They gave me a commendation." He slides into the chair, fingers moving automatically through the login sequence. "Speaking of paranoia, having a guest here feels wrong—maintenance checks are always done alone. That's protocol."

The screen flickers to life, seeking authentication. Alex enters his credentials one last time, wondering if the system can sense his betrayal through the keystrokes. "All yours," he says, standing to let Casey take his place. "Try not to break anything that isn't meant to be broken."

Casey's lips twitch as she settles into the chair. "No promises."

"Starting the upload," Casey murmurs, her fingers moving across the keyboard with precise efficiency. Data streams past in endless rivers of code on the screens above them. Somewhere in that digital flood are all the secrets they've come to expose—every lie, every manipulation, every carefully constructed piece of social engineering that keeps Valhalla Center under control.

Alex watches the door, his spine rigid with tension. In his pocket, the comm unit clicks three times: Talia warning them that someone has entered Building B. Not necessarily a problem—people do occasionally come to the secondary building—but it feeds the nagging worry about all those extra security sweeps. Like the system knows something's coming.

The servers hum around them, their tone almost musical. Alex remembers programming these same machines, teaching them to watch for patterns of dissent and flag any behavior that didn't match UmbraCorp's approved parameters. Now, they stand in the machine's temple, preparing to poison its digital bloodstream. The irony would be funny if it weren't so terrifying.

"Upload's at sixty percent," Casey whispers. Her face is bathed in the screen's blue glow, making her look almost ghostly. "You're sure about that fifteen-minute window?"

Alex nods, but his certainty feels shakier than it did this morning. "They always run deep system checks on Thursdays at 9 am. Been that way for years." He doesn't mention how they've been running extra checks all week, how each system notification has felt like a warning. "We should have plenty of time to—"

The lights flicker.

Alex freezes, his blood running cold. "That shouldn't happen."

"What shouldn't happen?" Casey's voice is sharp.

"Power fluctuation. The AI core has its own dedicated supply. It never fluctuates." He stares at the lights, mind racing. "Unless..."

The alarm blares, shattering the silence. Red lights flash along the walls, and a mechanical voice drones: "Intrusion detected. Sector E."

Casey curses under her breath. "Everyone? Move. Now."

They sprint for the elevators, Alex's mind racing. This is wrong—they should have had at least ten more minutes before the next security sweep. The corridors blur past, identical doors and identical walls designed to disorient intruders. But Alex knows this floor like he knows his own apartment; he's walked it too many times to get lost now.

"What's happening?" Casey demands as they round the corner to the elevator bank. "This isn't supposed to—"

"I know." Alex slams his hand against the call button. Nothing happens. He tries again, then swipes his ID card across the sensor. The panel stays dark. "Damn it. Security lockdown—elevators are the first thing they disable."

"Stairs?"

"Forty-seven floors down." Alex is already moving toward the emergency stairwell. "But my access should still work. They won't have flagged me yet—they're looking for unauthorized entry, not employees."

The stairwell door opens at his touch, confirming his theory. They start down, their footsteps echoing in the concrete shaft. The emergency lights cast everything in a dim red glow, making the descent feel like a journey into hell.

"Something triggered their systems early," Casey says between breaths as they take the stairs two at a time. "But what? Talia would have looped the camera feeds..."

"Maybe it wasn't the cameras." Alex's mind churns through possibilities as they descend. "All those extra security sweeps this week. Maybe they were updating their detection protocols. Maybe—" He cuts off as his comm unit crackles.

Through the static, they hear Marcus's voice: "—multiple breaches—they're not—" The transmission cuts out.

"Marcus?" Casey tries her own comm. Nothing but static. "Talia? Nicholas? Anyone?"

They reach the forty-second-floor landing. Alex's legs are already burning, but they can't slow down. His ID still works—the door opens when he swipes it—but for how long? How long before the system realizes he's moving through the building in a pattern that doesn't match any authorized response to a security alert?

"We need to know what's happening out there," Casey says as they cut through another identical corridor. "If they've found Talia and Marcus—"

"No point speculating," Alex interrupts, harsher than he means to. "We stick to the plan. Get down, get out, regroup at the safehouse."

But as they reach the next stairwell, his comm unit clicks in a pattern he doesn't recognize. Three quick, two slow, three quick. An SOS? Or something else? Without being able to reach the others, there's no way to know if the mission is blown or if this is just an equipment malfunction.

They keep moving down, floor after floor, the alarm's wail following them like a banshee. Alex's security clearance continues to work, each door opening to his touch, but the ease of their descent only increases his dread. It feels too easy...

The thirty-fifth-floor door opens to reveal a squad of security guards running past. Alex yanks Casey back into the stairwell before they're spotted. They wait, hearts pounding, as footsteps thunder past their hiding place.

"They're heading up," Alex whispers once the sound fades. "They don't know where we are. The system's just responding to multiple breaches—standard protocol is to sweep up from ground level."

"How long before they change strategy?"

"Depends if they're following basic containment procedures or..." He trails off, remembering all those extra security sweeps. Something about this feels wrong. They're missing something.

They emerge cautiously onto the thirty-fifth floor. The corridor is empty now, but Alex can hear distant shouting and orders being barked through radios. They move quickly but quietly, Alex leading them through a maze of service corridors he'd memorized years ago. Another door opens to his ID. Then another.

"You seem to know your way around the back routes pretty well," Casey observes as they slip through a maintenance area.

"I helped design the security systems. Had to know every possible entry and exit point." He pauses at a junction, checking both directions. "Also spent a lot of time avoiding my supervisor. Man loves surprise productivity checks."

A burst of static from their comms makes them both jump. Through the interference, they catch fragments: "—compromised—" and "—BOB—" before the signal dies completely.

Casey's face goes pale. "Did they say—"

"Move." Alex's voice is tight. If they've deployed BOB, everything's changed. "We need to get to the twentieth floor. There's a sky bridge to the adjacent building. It's our best shot now."

They push on, dropping through the levels as fast as they dare. Alex's mind races with each floor they descend. His credentials are still working, meaning they haven't identified him as the breach. Not yet. But BOB's involvement means they're taking this seriously. More seriously than a standard security breach would warrant.

What had they seen in the system? What triggered this response?

They continue down the stairwell at pace until a mechanical whir from below stops them cold. The sound echoes up the concrete shaft—something's coming up the stairs.

"Back, back," Alex hisses. He swipes his ID at the twenty-fourth-floor door. It opens, and they slip through just as the whirring grows louder.

The floor is dark except for the red emergency lights. They move quickly past empty cubicles toward the center of the building. "We can try the express elevators," Alex says. "They run on a separate system—"

His ID card fails at the security door. The panel flashes red: ACCESS DENIED.

"No." The word comes out as barely a whisper. He tries again. Red light. Again. Red light.

"Alex?" Casey's voice is tight.

"They know." His stomach drops as the reality hits him. "They know it's me." All those extra security sweeps this week—they'd been watching him. Waiting.

A drone zips around the corner, its red eye locking onto them instantly. They dive behind a row of desks as it opens fire with its containment rounds.

"Express elevators are out," Alex says, already scanning for options. "We need to get back to the stairs on the other side of the building." A plan forms in his mind—the building's symmetrical design working in their favor for once. "Through the break room, cut across the conference area—"

"Contact in Sector D," a mechanical voice broadcasts from the drone. "Targets identified. Deploying—"

Casey's thrown stapler catches it dead center, sending it spiraling into a wall with a satisfying crunch.

"Nice shot."

"Less talking, more running."

They sprint for the break room door. Behind them, they can hear heavy footsteps—guards, coming up fast. Alex's mind races through the building's layout. They can't go up, can't go down the way they came. But maybe...

"If we can get to the service elevator shaft," he says as they weave through tables, "there's maintenance access to—"

His comm unit crackles: "Alex." It's Talia's voice, strained. "They're herding you. Don't let them—" Static cuts her off.

They sprint for the break room door. Behind them, they can hear heavy footsteps—guards, coming up fast. Alex grabs a trash can as they run past, hurling it behind them. The crash and scatter of debris should slow pursuit, but more importantly, it feels good. After years of careful compliance, of perfect behavior, there's a fierce joy in finally fighting back.

The break room door won't accept his credentials anymore, but that doesn't matter. He rams a chair through the reinforced glass panel. It cracks but holds. The second hit brings it down.

"You know what?" Alex says as they climb through, ignoring the cuts from broken glass. "I've always hated this pretentious anti-shatter glass. Form over function, just like everything else here."

Two more drones appear at the far end of the break room. Casey's already grabbing coffee mugs from the counter, launching them with deadly accuracy. Alex upends an entire table, sending it skidding across the floor. The drones scatter, their targeting systems confused by the chaos of flying debris.

"The great thing about corporate break rooms," Alex says as they dash past the fallen drones, "is there's always something to throw."

His comm unit crackles: "Alex." It's Talia's voice, strained. "They're herding you. Don't let them—" Static cuts her off.

They burst through the far door into a long corridor lined with conference rooms. The glass walls that once represented UmbraCorp's "transparency" now work in their favor—they can see the drones and guards coming from either direction.

"In here," Alex yanks Casey into Conference Room C. Another place he'd spent countless hours designing systems meant to control people. The irony isn't lost on him as he starts pulling apart the video conferencing equipment.

"What are you—"

"Making a mess." He rips the cables free and hands one to Casey. "These power cables? Perfect for tangling drone rotors."

A crackle from his comm unit: "Nicholas here. We've got serious problems in the auxiliary building. They're not just trying to contain us, they're—" The transmission cuts off in a burst of static.

Through the glass walls, they see more guards approaching. But something's different about their movement—it's more purposeful and coordinated. They're not just sweeping the building anymore; they're following a plan.

"Talia was right," Casey says, readying her makeshift weapon. "They're pushing us somewhere."

"Then let's push back." Alex grabs a sleek conference chair—all ergonomic design and expensive materials—and hurls it through the glass wall. The crash is spectacular, sending shards everywhere. The guards dive for cover as Alex and Casey charge through the new exit.

They run past more conference rooms, past the framed corporate values that Alex had read every day without really seeing: Innovation. Control. Progress. He grabs a fire extinguisher from the wall, sprays it in a wide arc as two drones round the corner. The white powder blinds their sensors, sending them careening into each other.

But there's no satisfaction in the small victory. Something about the guards' coordinated movements, about Nicholas's cut-off warning, sends ice through Alex's veins. This isn't just about containing a security breach anymore.

A deep mechanical thrum reverberates through the building. Not from above or below—it seems to come from everywhere at once.

"That sound..." Casey's voice trails off.

"Yeah." Alex knows what it means. They all do. "Let's move."

The deep thrum grows stronger as they race through the building. It's not just sound anymore—Alex can feel it in his bones, in his teeth, a resonance that speaks to something primitive in his brain. Run. Hide. Survive.

They reach another stairwell access point. Alex doesn't bother trying his ID—just tackles the door panel, ripping it open to expose the wiring beneath.

Years of designing security systems taught him every weakness, every shortcut. The door clicks open.

"Going down?" he asks with grim humor.

"Wait." Casey grabs his arm. "Listen."

The stairwell echoes with sounds from above and below—footsteps, doors slamming, the whir of drones. But underneath it all, that mechanical thrum continues to build. It's closer now.

His comm unit splutters to life: "—multiple units—" Static. "—BOB isn't alone—" More static. Then Talia's voice, clear and urgent: "Alex, they're not just security units, they're—"

The transmission dies in a burst of feedback that makes them both wince.

"What did she mean, BOB isn't alone?" Casey asks.

Before Alex can answer, an impact shakes the building. Somewhere below them, metal screams against metal. The sound of something massive moving through walls rather than around them.

"They've upgraded him," Alex realizes. The extra security sweeps, the system updates—it wasn't just about finding infiltrators. They were preparing for this. "We need to—"

Another impact, closer this time. Concrete dust rains down from above.

"Options?" Casey asks, her voice steady despite everything.

Alex's mind races through the building's layout. They're on the twenty-second floor. Below them, something is systematically destroying everything in its path. Above them, guards and drones block any upward escape. And somewhere in this mess, their team is scattered, trying to survive.

His fingers brush the comm unit in his pocket. Somewhere out there, Nicholas and Sarah are fighting their own battles. Talia and Marcus might already be—

No. Focus.

"We need to reach the twentieth floor," he says. "There's a maintenance shaft that runs between the air handling units. If we can get there..."

They take the stairs at a dangerous pace, the impacts growing stronger and closer. At the twentieth-floor landing, Alex shoulders through the door into a utility corridor. The fluorescent lights flicker with each crash, casting juddering shadows on the concrete walls.

"This way." He leads them past hulking air handlers and tangles of pipes. "Maintenance shaft should be—"

The wall ahead explodes inward in a shower of concrete and steel. Through the dust, a familiar silhouette emerges—humanoid but wrong, its movements too precise, too mechanical. One of UmbraCorp's standard AI enforcers, all chrome and exposed hydraulics.

"They've been busy," Casey breathes.

Behind them, another impact. They spin to see a second enforcer unit stepping through a different wall, effectively boxing them in. These aren't BOB—they lack his eerily human appearance, his fluid grace. But they're dangerous enough.

The comm unit crackles. "Alex, Casey—we've got your location." Talia's voice is breathless. "We're coming to you."

"No!" Casey snaps into her comm. "Get out while you can—"

"Bit late for that," Nicholas's voice cuts in. "We've got BOB on our tail. Heading your way. Rather face him together than alone."

"You idiots," Casey mutters, but there's affection in her voice.

Alex spots the server room entrance behind the first enforcer. If they can just reach it... "That room," he says quietly to Casey. "It's got independent power, security overrides. If we can get in there—"

"We can make a stand," she finishes. "Better than being hunted through the building."

The enforcers advance in perfect synchronization, herding them exactly where Alex suspects they're meant to go. But with BOB driving the others toward them too, maybe that's not such a bad thing. The guilt that's been his constant companion since joining Voxx Pop twists in his gut—these people are risking everything because of systems he helped create. Systems he can now help them destroy.

The standard enforcers advance with mechanical precision - threatening but predictable, exactly the kind of security measure Alex had helped implement. The kind of system that worked through intimidation rather than true power. But BOB... Alex's breath catches at the thought of facing him again.

"Through here!" Alex shouts as they dive past the enforcers, rolling into the server room. The familiar hum of processors fills the air, banks of equipment stretching into shadows. How many hours had he spent in rooms like this, perfecting systems meant to control and contain? The guilt rises like bile in his throat.

Casey's already moving to the central console. "Can you seal those doors?"

"Better." Alex yanks open an access panel, exposing the wiring he knows by heart. "I can trigger the fire suppression protocols. Create a barrier—"

A crash from the corridor behind them. Shouts. The sound of running feet. Then Talia and Marcus burst through the doorway, Nicholas right behind them. And in the hallway beyond, a shadow moves. Fluid. Graceful. Terrifyingly human.

"Seal it!" Casey barks. "Seal it now!"

But Alex's hands freeze on the wires as BOB steps into view. Not chrome and hydraulics like the standard enforcers. Not obvious machinery. Instead, a perfect mimicry of human form, right up until you meet those red eyes. Eyes that now lock onto Alex with terrible recognition.

Chapter 17

Tracing Terror

The room feels impossibly small as BOB strides forward, his hulking frame glinting in the dim light. His movements are unnervingly smooth—each step deliberate, functional, and calculated. It doesn't help, of course, that he's virtually unkillable.

Alex ducks behind a server rack, his breath catching in his throat as BOB's red sensors sweep the room, locking on the nearest target.

"Keep moving!" Casey barks through the comms, her voice rising over the blaring alarms.

Alex glances around the room, his mind racing. Talia is crouched near an exposed access panel, frantically trying to re-route a power source, while Marcus scrambles to set up a barricade with toppled server towers.

BOB moves faster than Alex remembers—too fast. They've upgraded him. A blade-like appendage extends from his arm, slicing cleanly through a metal support beam as though it were paper. Sparks shower the room, and the walls tremble under the force of his blows.

"Alex!" Casey's voice cuts through the chaos. "Any bright ideas?"

Alex's gaze darts to a cluster of exposed wiring near the base of a collapsed server tower. An idea does form—it's not bright, though; it's rough and desperate.

"Talia, can you overload the circuit for that section?" Alex says, pointing toward the wires.

Talia's head snaps up, expression grim but focused. "You want to fry the floor?"

"Exactly. Force him to recalculate his footing. It'll buy us time."

Talia's face says she doesn't think it'll work, but she doesn't argue. Her hands move quickly, connecting wires and redirecting power, changing the circuitry.

"Everyone, clear the area!" Alex shouts.

BOB advances, his sensors locking onto Alex. Just as the towering figure steps onto the electrified section, Talia slams down on the switch.

The room erupts in a burst of light. Electricity courses through the floor, crackling and arcing across BOB's frame. For a moment, he freezes, his movements jerky and unnatural as his systems struggle to adapt.

"Move!" Casey shouts, grabbing Alex by the arm and pulling him toward the next corridor.

The group sprints, the sound of BOB's machinations growing louder behind them.

The corridor leading to the Mainframe is narrower than Alex expected. The walls are lined with glowing blue panels that pulse faintly.

"We're close," Alex says, his voice tight.

"Good," Casey replies, though her tone is anything but relieved. "How much time do you need to finish the upload?"

"Five minutes. Maybe less."

"Five minutes we don't have," Talia mutters.

"Better idea? Didn't think so." Casey snaps back.

Ahead, the corridor opens into a cavernous chamber. The Mainframe dominates the space; it's a sleek, glass-enclosed structure that houses rows of servers stretching toward the ceiling.

"Hold up right here," Casey orders, motioning for the group to fan out.

Alex moves to the Mainframe terminal, pulling the drive containing the final payload from his bag. His fingers tremble as he connects it to the system, the screen flooding with lines of code as the upload begins.

"We're exposed," Chameleon warns.

"We're always exposed," Casey snaps back, her eyes scanning the chamber for movement.

The comms crackle and a static-laced voice breaks through: "He's coming."

***

The warning comes too late. BOB bursts into the chamber, his frame glinting with fresh scorch marks but otherwise unscathed—his upgrades must've included a mechanical version of battlefield medicine. His blade slices through the air as the group scatters.

"Keep him away from the Mainframe!" Casey shouts.

Alex presses himself against the terminal, his hands flying across the keyboard. The upload bar crawls forward, agonizingly slow.

BOB lunges toward the terminal, but Nicholas steps into his path, raising his weapon.

"Hey, Tin Man!" Nicholas shouts, his voice steady despite the chaos. "You going to Oz or are you lookin' for me?"

BOB's sensors lock onto Nicholas, and the hulking machine pivots toward him.

"Nicholas, don't!" Alex shouts.

But Nicholas doesn't hesitate, not for a second. He charges forward, firing off a burst of shots that ping harmlessly against BOB's armor. It's a distraction—one that costs him dearly.

BOB's blade sweeps out, catching Nicholas in the chest. The older man stumbles, fresh blood spreading across his shirt as he collapses to the floor.

"Nicholas!" Alex's voice breaks. His fingers freeze on the keyboard for half a second—a stupid, useless instinct to move and help, to do *something*. But Casey grabs his arm, forcing him to stay at the terminal.

"Focus!" she snaps. "We can't lose this now."

Alex's vision blurs, but he keeps typing, his fingers moving on autopilot. The upload bar ticks forward.

Behind him, Nicholas gasps out his final words: *Make it count.*

The upload completes with a low chime, the terminal screen flashing green. Alex exhales shakily, his hands falling to his sides.

"It's done," he says, his voice barely audible.

The broadcast begins immediately, overriding every network, feed, and screen. The cavernous chamber is bathed in shifting light as the President's face appears, his calm, calculated demeanor filling the space.

The group watches in silence as the clips play: Klepton addressing members of his inner circle. "The masses are predictable. Obedient. They want stability, not freedom. Keep them fed just enough to survive, and they won't just do what we tell them; they'll thank us for it."

A hidden camera captures a lavish dinner party. The President raises a glass, laughing with his peers. "They're rationing water, and we're debating wine pairings. You can't make this stuff up!"

Footage showing BOB and the Conformity Corps suppressing protests with brutal efficiency. Tear gas, fragmentation grenades, and batons fill the frame as dissenters are dragged away, their screams haunting.

A private conversation between the President and a general. "It's all about currency; if they rebel, we remind them of the cost of disobedience. Their hunger will silence them—it always has, and it always will."

The broadcast cuts to live footage of the rebellion beginning to spread.

Casey steps forward, her voice quiet but firm. "We did it."

But Alex can't feel the triumph. Not when Nicholas is dead.

"Come on, let's move," Casey says, her tone leaving no room for argument.

The group turns to leave, the sound of BOB's systems rebooting echoing behind them.

The group moves through the dimly lit corridors, every step feeling heavier than the last. The sound of BOB's systems rebooting echoes behind them, his mechanical growl growing louder with every second.

"We're not gonna outrun him," Marcus says. "You know that, right?"

Alex glances back at him, his stomach turning. "What are you saying?"

Marcus's lips press into a thin line. He looks at the team, and the weight of his decision is clear in his eyes.

"I'm saying you don't need all of us to finish this," Marcus replies.

"No," Alex says, his voice rising in protest. "Absolutely not. We've already lost Nicholas; we're not losing you, too."

"Listen to me," Marcus says.

He steps closer, gripping Alex by the shoulder. "This isn't about me. It never was! It's about the movement. About the *world*. If we don't stop him here, no one's getting out alive."

Casey's gaze locks with Marcus's, and an understanding passes between them. "What's the plan?" she asks.

Marcus pulls a small device from his jacket. It's a remote detonator. "There's a maintenance shaft two floors below us. If I can get him down there, I can collapse the whole section. It won't kill him, but it'll bury him long enough for you to escape."

Alex shakes his head, his hands balling into fists. "No. There has to be another way."

"There isn't," Marcus says, his voice softening. "This is what I signed up for. What we *all* signed up for. I don't have a family anymore. My closest friends are the people within this square mile. It's okay. I made my peace with an ending like this."

The sound of BOB's footsteps grows louder, his presence looming just out of sight.

Marcus pats Alex on the shoulder, offering him a weary smile. "You've got this, Alex. Finish the fight. You're stronger than you think."

Before Alex can protest further, Marcus turns and sprints toward the approaching sound of BOB, his figure disappearing into the shadows.

The group keeps moving, but Alex can't stop himself from looking back, his heart pounding as Marcus's voice crackles through the comms.

"All right, you oversized toaster. Let's dance."

The sounds of the confrontation echo through the comms—gunfire, the screech of metal, and BOB's staticky noises.

Alex imagines Marcus standing his ground against the towering machine. It's a horrible picture that he immediately tries to unsee.

A low rumble reverberates through the facility, followed by a deafening explosion that shakes the walls. The lights flicker briefly before stabilizing, and the comms go silent.

For a moment, no one speaks.

"Holy...he actually did it," Casey says finally, her voice quiet and steady. "He bought us the time we need."

Alex doesn't respond. His hands tremble as he grips the comms device, the enormity of Marcus's sacrifice settling over him. It's something he knows he'll never fully come to terms with.

They push forward, reaching the entrance to the abandoned maglev tunnels—hidden beneath layers of urban decay. The station is a relic of the past, its entrance half-buried in rubble, rusted tracks stretching into darkness. The scent of stagnant water lingers in the stale air. Somewhere above, sirens wail through Valhalla Center's perpetual twilight as authorities tighten their grip on the city.

They're battered, bloodied, and fewer in number than when they started. Alex glances around at the remaining members of Voxx Pop, their faces pale and etched with grief in the dim emergency lighting that still functions down here. The weight of loss hangs over them all.

Movement from another tunnel entrance makes them all tense, but then Sarah emerges from the shadows, looking as battered as the rest of them.

"Thank god," Casey breathes, pulling her into a quick embrace. "We lost contact with you after—"

"An explosion sealed off the corridor, so I couldn't get out," Sarah says, catching her breath. "Had to find another way out through the maintenance tunnels." Her eyes scan their reduced group, and Alex sees the moment she realizes who's missing. "Nicholas? Marcus?"

The silence that follows is answer enough, but Casey speaks anyway, her voice rough. "Nicholas...BOB got him. While we were uploading the data. And Marcus..." She swallows hard. "He gave us a chance to escape. Collapsed the maintenance shaft on BOB."

Sarah's face goes pale, grief and shock warring in her expression. She'd worked with Nicholas for years, Alex remembers. Had been part of Voxx Pop long before he joined.

"They made it count," Talia says quietly. "The broadcast went out. Everyone's seeing the truth."

Casey pauses at a junction in the tunnels, her gaze scanning the darkness ahead. "We need to move. UmbraCorp's gonna have every drone in the sector looking for us."

"We can't just leave them," Alex says, his voice raw.

Casey turns to him, her expression hard but not unkind. "He knew what he was doing. And *we* are going to honor him by honoring that—and staying alive."

As they regroup, the glow of screens illuminates the night sky. The broadcast is still playing, its message cutting through the noise of the world.

The news reports haven't caught up yet. The city is eerily silent. The government will try to suppress this and control the narrative. For now, most people are still processing what they've just seen.

But cracks are forming. Alex knows it's only a matter of time.

***

The group moves deeper into the tunnels, the air growing colder the further they descend. Their footsteps echo against steel and concrete, swallowed by the endless dark stretching ahead.

Casey leads the way, her pace brisk but tense. The tension in her shoulders is visible, even in the darkness. She knows these tunnels, knows which ones are safest, which ones the state might have sealed. Behind her, Alex trails in silence, his thoughts spiraling with every step.

He can still see Nicholas' face. The way he stood in BOB's path without hesitation, those last words still echoing in Alex's mind on a loop: *Make it count.*

Alex's hands tremble as he grips the strap of his bag, the weight of the mission pressing down on him. He glances at the others—what's left of them. Talia limps beside him. Sarah clutches her side.

After what feels like an eternity, Casey finally calls for a halt. They collapse against the tunnel walls, backs pressing into cold metal and cracked tile, too drained to argue.

Alex sits apart from the others with his back pressed against the cold metal wall. He stares at his hands, smeared with grease and blood, and thinks of Nicholas.

Nicholas, who had every reason to give up but chose to fight. A guy who had made the ultimate sacrifice—not out of duty, but out of true belief. It was sad and inspiring.

For years, Alex had told himself he was powerless, just another cog in the machine. He had buried himself in work, in routine, convincing himself that survival was enough and staying quiet was the only way to ensure he could protect Mila and Jackson.

But Nicholas hadn't stayed quiet. He had faced the impossible, knowing he wouldn't survive, because he believed in something bigger than himself.

And now, Alex was still alive. Still breathing.

Still running.

His survival wasn't just an accident. It was a responsibility.

Nicholas' sacrifice wasn't just for the group—it was for Mila, for Jackson, for everyone who didn't fully realize they were living in a cage.

Alex swallows hard, the full realization slowly settling over him. For years, he had been passive, waiting—for the system to collapse, for someone else to act, for change to come without his hands being the ones to force it. And what had that waiting given him?

Nothing.

"No more," he whispers under his breath.

Casey approaches, her boots scuffing lightly against the concrete. She doesn't sit; she just leans against a support beam, her arms crossed tightly over her chest.

"They're looking to you now, you know," she says, nodding toward the rest of the group.

Alex glances at the others, their faces weary and hollow but watching him nonetheless. He feels the weight of their gazes and their unspoken hope.

"I don't know what I'm doing," Alex admits.

Casey exhales, her expression softening slightly. "None of us does, Alex. Voxx Pop wasn't born out of some grand strategy. We started with nothing but desperation and a refusal to roll over. It doesn't matter if you don't know. What matters is that you keep going."

Alex looks up at her. "How do you do it? How do you keep everyone together?"

Casey shrugs. "By not thinking about it. If I stop to think, I'll fall apart. And we can't afford that. Especially not now."

She pauses, her gaze shifting to the horizon. "Nicholas knew that. Marcus knew it, too. They didn't stop, and neither will we."

As dawn breaks, the group gathers around a small portable screen salvaged from their escape. The glow of the broadcast is steady, showing glimpses of the world they've just begun to change.

The rebellion is reaching more people than they realized. It's too soon for full-scale uprisings, but the ripples are spreading.

A handful of government feeds have been hijacked, and rogue broadcasters are dissecting the leaked files, forcing people to confront the truth. Underground networks are alight with messages, encrypted chatter moving faster than Umbra-Corp's censors can contain.

But a few hundred "glitchers" aren't going to initiate real change, and not all the news is hopeful.

In some sectors, riot squads are already in formation, black-armored enforcers moving through the streets, locking down transportation hubs, and dragging dissenters into waiting transports. But resistance is there, too.

Somewhere in another city, surveillance drones have been torn from the sky, their shattered remains littering the streets. Elsewhere, ration warehouses smolder, smoke rising like dark pillars against the skyline.

Talia shakes her head. "Never takes them long, does it?"

"They're not acting from a place of control," Casey murmurs, her gaze fixed on the screen. "They're scared." She tilts her head slightly. "And they should be."

Alex watches in silence.

The rebellion is alive but fragile. A spark, not yet a flame. And UmbraCorp will do everything in its power to snuff it out before it spreads.

The screen flickers again, then fades to black.

One by one, the others begin packing up, their movements slow, heavy with exhaustion.

Alex lingers, his gaze drifting toward the far end of the tunnel, where the first light of dawn spills through the cracks in the crumbling infrastructure. The city above is still locked under its own weight, its people caught between fear and awakening.

He thinks of Mila and Jackson. Of their faces, their voices. Of the world he wants them to live in—a world where they don't have to ration every meal and don't have to fear the knock of an enforcer at the door.

Alex's resolve hardens. He pushes to his feet, his eyes meeting Casey's. "We'll finish what we started," he says, his voice steady.

Casey studies him for a moment, then nods in approval.

"Damn right, we will."

Chapter 18

Identity

The city feels larger at night, its sprawling streets illuminated by neon lights and flickering holograms that cast shifting shadows against the steel and glass buildings.

Alex keeps his head down, his hood pulled tight, but his heart pounds with every step. He shouldn't be alone. He was just with the others, moving through the tunnels, still reeling from what they had lost. But as soon as they surfaced in a lower sector, it became clear—he couldn't stay with them.

The others had some chance of disappearing back into the city's underbelly. Alex didn't. His face is everywhere.

Not just a single image, but dozens. His biometric profile. Age-enhanced and disguise-predicted versions of him. Surveillance algorithms had worked at inhuman speed, rendering potential variations—him with dyed hair, with facial modifications, with added weight. They were sparing nothing.

On the corner of 7th and Locke, an enormous digital billboard flickers to life. His own face towers over him, so large it makes him feel momentarily unsteady. The animation is seamless, his image turning slowly as if scanning the crowd. Watching.

Beneath it, bold red text blares:

"WANTED: ALEX VANGUARD. REWARD: 10,000 CREDITS."

A pit forms in his stomach. The display isn't just an image—it's a living simulation. The digital Alex blinks, and tilts his head, his mouth moving in a looped, monotone warning:

"Alex Vanguard is a fugitive. Report any sightings immediately."

He ducks into the shadows, his breath shallow, trying to slow his heart. They know. Not just that someone infiltrated UmbraCorp—but that it was him. And if they know it was him...they know who he loves.

Mila. Jackson.

His hands tighten into fists. He should be heading straight for them, but that's exactly what UmbraCorp is counting on. They'll be watching his home. His habits. Every place he's ever gone. Going to them now would be a death sentence—for all of them.

Across the street, a 3D hologram flickers to life above a plaza fountain. It hovers six feet in the air, rotating so his likeness can be seen from every angle.

People stop to watch. Some glance around nervously, their gazes skimming the crowd. Others pull out devices, scanning the hologram to access the reward details.

Ten thousand credits.

Enough to feed a family for a year. Enough to tempt even the people who might hesitate before turning someone in.

A drone zips overhead, its red sensor light sweeping the alley. Alex presses himself against the cold brick wall, clutching the Voxx Pop jammer hidden beneath his jacket. The device hums against his palm, scrambling the tracking chip embedded in his forearm—his only defense against being instantly located.

The drone hovers, its sensors twitching, recalibrating. Too long. Alex holds his breath. Then, it darts off toward the square. e doesn't move until the sound of its whirring fades completely.

Alex pulls his hood lower, forcing himself back into the flow of the city's underbelly. The streets are alive with faces—hungry, tired, angry—but no one stops him.

Not yet, at least.

But he knows this city. He knows what fear does to people. Someone will recognize him soon. He needs a plan. And he needs it fast.

***

The subway station feels like it exists on a different planet. Alex steps through the rusted turnstile, his movements careful as he descends the cracked, graffiti-covered steps. The air grows colder the deeper he goes, the smell of mildew clinging to the damp walls.

It's quiet down here, the chaos of the city muffled by layers of concrete and decay. But something feels wrong.

At the bottom of the steps, Alex pauses, his eyes narrowing. The faintest glint of light flickers from the far end of the tunnel. It's not the flicker of a broken overhead bulb—it's deliberate. Controlled.

He moves cautiously, and his footsteps are light against the cracked tiles. The sound of machinery reaches his ears—someone is here. The tunnel opens into a vast underground chamber, and Alex freezes. It's like stepping into another world.

Rows of hydroponic gardens glow with pale green light, their roots dangling in water channels. A solar-powered generator sits quietly in the corner, its improvised design cobbled together from salvaged parts. Shelves line the walls, stacked with canned goods, medical supplies, and tools.

People move through the area. Their movements are efficient but unhurried. A teenager hauls a crate of vegetables across the room while an older man tinkers with a piece of machinery.

Alex takes a step forward, and the room reacts instantly.

A voice cuts through the sounds of activity. "Stop right there."

Alex freezes, his eyes darting toward the sound. A woman steps into view, her posture relaxed, but her eyes show something far more intentional. She's middle-aged, with a lean build and silver-streaked hair tied back in a loose braid. Her face is lined but striking, her expression calm yet commanding.

"Hands where I can see them." Her tone makes it clear it's not a request.

Alex raises his hands slowly. "I'm not here to cause trouble."

"Then why are you here?" Her eyes narrow.

"I need to lay low," Alex admits. "Just...for a little bit."

Her gaze flicks over him, assessing. "What are you hiding from?"

Alex hesitates, glancing back toward the tunnel. "Pretty sure you already know."

A humorless smile tugs at her lips. "Alex Vanguard."

It wasn't a question.

"That's me," Alex says, lowering his hands slightly. "But I'm not here to drag you into anything, okay? I promise. I just need somewhere to plant myself and stay out of sight."

The woman studies him for a long moment with an unreadable expression. Part of Alex is waiting for a bullet to his leg or some other non-fatal injury; from what the signs say, he's worth more alive than dead.

Then she motions for him to follow. "Come with me," she says. "Let's talk."

The woman leads Alex to a quieter section of the chamber, where a worn wooden table sits surrounded by mismatched chairs. She gestures for him to sit, taking the seat across from him.

"I'm Harmony," she says, as if they were two normal people in normal circumstances, though neither one of which is the case.

Alex nods. "So...you run this place?"

"Something like that," Harmony replies. Just like Casey, Harmony possesses a quiet authority that commands respect without ever asking for it. "We've been here a long time, back to a time before the world started noticing people like you."

Alex glances around, taking in the setup of their underground sanctuary. "You've built all this yourself?"

Harmony's lips twitch into a smile. "We didn't have much choice. UmbraCorp doesn't like people who fall off the grid, now do they?"

Alex wants to ask more, but her eyes warn him not to pry. "So why take the risk?"

Harmony studies him for a moment. "Because you're not the first to fight the good fight and get the bill. And you sure as hell won't be the last."

She doesn't ask why he fought. She doesn't need to. Alex isn't sure what that leaves him with. Gratitude? Responsibility? Or just the gnawing weight of everything that's happened? But before he can find an answer, a wiry man drops a bundle of scrap into his lap that Alex recognizes as a mostly dismantled drone.

"Hope you like working for your keep." His angular features are half-lit by the glow of a nearby light. "I'm Kade."

Alex sits cross-legged on the floor, holding a battered screwdriver in his hand. Kade crouches over the dismantled drone, his fingers working with quick, practiced precision. He prods at a tangle of frayed wires, then tugs carefully at a thin filament in the drone's core.

"This one's an older model," he mutters. "Heat sensors are garbage, but if you strip this..."

He slides the filament free with a controlled pull, triumphantly holding it up. It shimmers in the dim light, so fine it looks like it might snap if handled wrong.

"Boom," Kade says with a smug grin. "Infrared tracker. Can pick up body heat from two klicks out if you wire it right."

Alex takes the filament carefully, turning it between his fingers. Lighter than a thread, but strong. His hands move hesitantly at first, unsure of the right pressure, but muscle memory kicks in.

"Not like that," Kade snaps, pointing. "You'll fry the whole damn board if you twist it too tight. Loosen your grip."

Alex adjusts, forcing his hands to stay steady. The tension eases, the connection slotting into place with a near-silent click.

Kade grunts, watching over his shoulder. Then he exhales, a grudging smirk tugging at his mouth.

"Huh," he muses. "So you've handled guts before. That's nice. You're not entirely hopeless."

Alex doesn't look up; he just keeps stripping the filament.

Kade snorts. "Not bad, Vanguard. Thought I'd have to spell out which end of the screwdriver to hold."

Alex doesn't bother responding, but a realization creeps in as he works. At UmbraCorp, everything was structured. Tech had a purpose, a function, and a place. He had built things that reinforced the system, made it more efficient, and made it more compliant. Here, he's tearing things apart to make them do what they were never meant to.

Later, Alex crouches beside a cluttered workbench, its surface covered in scavenged junk: old circuit boards, frayed wiring, shattered tablet screens. Harmony watches over him, her eyes scanning his movements.

"We don't buy, and we sure as hell don't steal—we salvage," she says, flipping a handheld device over in her palm. "Everything the surface world has thrown away, we've pulled back into service."

Alex frowns, turning over a battered power cell in his hands. "How do you know what's worth saving?"

"You learn by breaking it first."

She hands him a half-dismantled drone, its innards exposed like a dissected insect. "Think you can turn this into a pulse blocker?"

Alex hesitates, his mind ticking through possible configurations. "I've built jammers before, but this—"

"Isn't about building," Harmony interrupts. "It's about seeing what's already there. This isn't a lab, Vanguard. Learn to make what you need from what you've got."

Alex works quietly, sweat forming on his brow as he strips wires, reconfigures circuits, and splices the drone's sensor array into a makeshift emitter. Harmony doesn't offer help, only terse corrections when he fumbles.

When the device comes to life, emitting a soft pulse, Alex breathes a sigh of relief. Harmony nods approvingly. "Not bad for a surface dweller."

***

The tunnels stretch endlessly, the walls closing in like the throat of some forgotten beast. Alex follows Harmony's lantern light, its glow barely pushing back the darkness. The air is thick with damp earth and decay, heavy with the weight of a city built on top of its own past.

His fingers tighten around the Voxx Pop jammer in his jacket pocket. It hums softly, disrupting tracking signals and making him invisible to every smart system scanning the city above. But it also means he cannot know if Mila and Jackson are safe.

No messages. No updates. No way to reach them.

He doesn't even know if he should try. If UmbraCorp has already figured out he's the infiltrator, they know exactly who to look for. The thought coils tight in his chest, a slow, suffocating panic.

"This city was built in layers," Harmony says, breaking through his thoughts. He forces himself to focus.

"The surface is the newest, but down here..." She runs a hand along the wall, her fingers brushing across faded lettering.

"...this is old blood. Forgotten veins of the city."

Alex feels like he's walking through the bones of something that should have died long ago.

At a junction where several tunnels converge, Harmony stops. The walls are marked with cryptic symbols—slashes, arrows, jagged lines—each one carved by hands long gone.

Alex runs his fingers across one. "What do these mean?"

"Directions," Harmony replies. "Warnings. Maps. Some of them are ours. Some of them... older."

She kneels, pointing to a jagged arrow etched deep into the floor. "This means safe passage. Unless you're being tracked, of course."

Alex glances over his shoulder, half-expecting to see a drone waiting in the shadows. That paranoia doesn't go away. "How do you know all this?"

Harmony's eyes are unreadable in the dim light. "I've been down here long enough to learn."

"You want to survive?" she continues. "Don't just learn the landscape; master it. Every corner, blind turn, and unmarked exit could mean the difference between life and death. These tunnels aren't just hiding places, Vanguard. They're weapons. And we use every weapon we can get our hands on."

As they move deeper, Alex starts to see the tunnels differently. He'd spent years designing security for places like UmbraCorp, thinking like an engineer, someone who trusted barriers and surveillance and assumed control was absolute.

But these tunnels mock the idea of control. They exist beyond the reach of smart grids, security checkpoints, and retinal scans. They are older than the systems that try to control them.

Harmony doesn't move through them like she's hiding. She moves like she owns them.

Alex realizes that his way of thinking has left him vulnerable in ways he never understood. UmbraCorp had given him a map of the world and a structure to understand it, but he had never questioned the ground beneath his feet until now.

When they finally emerge into a vast, cavernous space, Alex hesitates, not because of the space itself but because he's no longer sure where he belongs in it.

The chamber is filled with flickering lanterns, scavenged technology, and the sound of people working with their hands. It's a world built from things that were never meant to last.

And yet...it has lasted. More than the world he came from ever will.

Back in the main chamber, Alex does what he can to earn his keep. He's not here to be trained but to lay low. But he's not going to sit around and do nothing.

So when Kade hands him a screwdriver and jerks his head toward a pile of salvaged drones, he gets to work.

"Strip them for anything useful," Kade mutters, already elbow-deep in rewiring a sensor array. "Leave the boards intact if you can."

Alex doesn't ask questions. The movements are familiar; disassembling circuits and testing connections, but the purpose is different.

He watches as Kade rigs a sensor to a homemade tripwire, crude but effective.

"If a drone locks onto you," Kade mutters, half to himself, "force it into a blind spot." He points to a small, modified disperser. "Obscure its thermal scan, force it to rely on visual tracking, then lead it somewhere it can't move."

Alex makes a mental note.

Harmony and a few others assemble a barricade from scrap metal and furniture at another table. It's not a solid defense—it's a funnel, forcing anyone who enters into a kill zone.

"This isn't about strength," Harmony says, tossing a frayed rope over the structure to reinforce it. "Prey doesn't win by fighting. It wins by being unpredictable."

Alex gets it. They don't fight like an army. They fight like something that refuses to be caught.

By the time the work slows down, his muscles ache, his fingers are raw, and his mind is still racing.

The preppers drift off to their sleeping quarters, but Alex stays behind, sitting on a worn crate, turning the Voxx Pop jammer over in his hands.

He's learned more in a few hours here than he ever did working inside the system. And yet...

None of it helps him reach Mila and Jackson. No amount of barricades, traps, or sensor tricks will help him determine whether they're safe.

Is he fighting to survive, like Harmony? Or is he still fighting to change the world?

"You can't stay here forever."

Alex looks up to see Harmony leaning against the wall, her arms crossed.

"I know," Alex says quietly.

Harmony steps closer, pulling something from her pocket. It's a compact signal scrambler, more advanced than the one Alex carries.

"Take this," she says, holding it out. "It'll give you a fighting chance."

Alex hesitates, then takes the device, feeling its cool surface in his hand. "Thank you," he says.

Harmony shrugs. "Don't thank me. Just don't waste it."

Chapter 19

Seeds of Rebellion

The low vibration of machinery carries through the underground chamber as Harmony shakes Alex awake. The soft green glow of the hydroponic lights silhouettes her figure.

"Wake up," she says. "It's time."

Alex pushes himself upright, the stiff cot creaking beneath him. The air is damp, tinged with the earthy scent of soil and traces of metal. He rubs his face, still groggy, as Harmony places a folded scrap of paper in his hand.

"Coordinates," she explains. "It's a Voxx Pop safe house. A day's travel if you move fast and don't get yourself caught."

He unfolds the paper, scanning the scrawled numbers. "How do you know it's still safe?"

Harmony leans against the doorway, crossing her arms. "I don't. But Casey reached out through emergency channels. They wouldn't risk it unless it mattered."

Alex nods, folding the paper and tucking it into his pocket. There's tension in the air between them, unspoken but undeniable.

Harmony studies him for a long moment. "You've learned enough to make it out there," she says finally. "Trust what you've learned. And don't second-guess yourself."

Alex reaches for his pack, slinging it over his shoulder. "Thank you."

Harmony waves him off but then stops. "Never forget: the people you fight for are the ones who'll keep you alive."

***

The tunnels stretch endlessly, their walls streaked with grime and faded graffiti. Alex walks cautiously, his flashlight casting a thin beam that cuts through the murky air. Symbols left by the preppers mark the way forward: arrows scratched into the walls, crude maps carved into the concrete.

At each junction, Alex pauses to listen. The silence presses in around him, broken only by the occasional sound of dripping water or skittering of rats. He grips the handle of his knife tightly, his mind running through Harmony's drills.

When he finally reaches an access hatch, he stops. He presses his ear to the cool metal, straining to hear any movement above. Satisfied that it's clear, he pushes the hatch open.

The city's outskirts are a wasteland of cracked asphalt and abandoned buildings. Alex keeps low as he moves, sticking to alleyways and shadows. The oppressive stillness of the streets is punctuated by the glow of patrol drones that sweep overhead, their searchlights cutting through the darkness.

The first checkpoint appears—a barricade in the middle of a main road. Alex ducks behind a dumpster, peering out at the scene. Two enforcers in sleek uniforms stand beneath a surveillance drone, their weapons glinting in the artificial light.

A man approaches the checkpoint cautiously, holding a tattered bag. Alex watches as the enforcers interrogate him.

"You've been in Sector D," one of them says, scanning the man's ID chip. "Who did you speak with?"

"I—I didn't talk to anyone," the man stammers. "I was just getting supplies."

The enforcers exchange a look. Alex doesn't wait to see what happens next. He backs away, slipping into a narrow alley.

The further Alex moves into the city, the more signs he sees of UmbraCorp's crackdown:

His face looms over an intersection on a digital billboard, the image unnervingly lifelike. The words "WANTED: ALEX VANGUARD" flash in bold red letters, followed by a reward amount that feels obscene.

Posters and holograms along the streets repeat the same propaganda slogans: "Compliance Is Freedom," "Report Dissidents Immediately," and "Safety Through Obedience."

A group of scavengers lingers near an abandoned market, their equipment cobbled together but dangerous-looking. One of them clutches a handheld scanner, its screen flickering erratically.

Alex realizes that they're probably bounty hunters. Not that he can blame them. His dad used to say, "Everyone wants more money; that's why it's called money."

He moves carefully. By the time Alex reaches the safe house, his nerves feel frayed. The building is an unremarkable apartment complex. Its walls are weathered and stained, and the windows are covered with thick sheets of plastic.

Alex glances around, scanning for any signs of surveillance before approaching the door. A Voxx Pop emblem is scratched into the frame, barely visible in the dim light.

He knocks twice, waits, then knocks again. The door cracks open, revealing a well-built man with a cautious gaze. A pistol rests in a holster at his side.

"What happened to the barracuda?" the man asks.

Alex closes his eyes, racking his brain; it's one of the codes that Casey taught him.

"It swam backward into the reef," Alex replies, hoping he remembered correctly.

The man studies him, nods, and steps back, fully opening the door. "Come in. And keep it quiet."

The inside of the safehouse is small but clean. The air is warm and thick with the scent of coffee and something herbal. Blankets and thick sheets cover the windows, muting the glow of the city outside. Stacks of organized-looking ration packs, canned food, and bottled water fill one corner.

A small sofa sits near a heating unit, and a folding table holds a collection of radios and handheld screens. Their screens are dim but active. Against the far wall, a neatly folded blanket and a set of toy blocks sit. The sight hits Alex harder than he expects.

There's life here. Not just survival—actual life.

The man studies him more closely now, his gaze traveling over Alex's filthy clothes and the exhaustion on his face.

"Who sent you?"

"Casey."

"We've had a lot of movement lately," the man says. "Who are you looking for?"

Alex was ready for a challenge. Ready for a fight. But he wasn't ready for that question. His throat goes tight. "...Mila. And Jackson."

The guard searches his face again, and this time, something clicks. The man motions toward a narrow hallway. "They're in the back."

Alex can't breathe.

They're in the back.

Alex is still waiting for something else. For a condition or a clarification. A 'but.' Not just 'they're here'. He should go to them, but his body won't cooperate. What if it's not them? Maybe the guard misspoke?

What if it's just their belongings, a sign that they'd been here, but left, taken, or worse?

He forces himself to take a breath. Forces himself to move. What if Mila is furious at him? He's sure that Jackson will be. What can he tell them? He didn't tell Mila anything or how long he'd be gone.

He hesitates for a moment before forcing himself to move toward the door.

***

The door creaks slightly as Alex pushes it open. Mila looks up first. She's sitting on a couch, her hands wrapped tightly around a steaming mug of tea. Her face is pale, her eyes puffy and red, but the moment she sees Alex, her entire body stiffens as though she doesn't quite believe it's him.

"Alex," she whispers, her voice cracking. "You're…"

"Alive?"

"I was going to say 'here,' but sure, alive is good, too."

Before he knows it, she's on her feet, crossing the room. Her mug clatters to the ground, spilling across the floor, but neither of them notices.

She throws her arms around him, clinging tightly, and Alex feels her trembling against him. He stands frozen for a moment, guilt and relief warring in his chest, before his arms come up and wrap around her.

"I'm sorry," he whispers, his voice breaking. "I should've…"

Mila doesn't respond right away. She presses her face into his shoulder, her breath hitching as she starts to cry.

"We're here, and we're safe. That's all that matters. It's about what comes next."

Alex closes his eyes, swallowing against the lump in his throat. He wants to say something, but everything feels inadequate. Instead, he just holds her, letting her tears soak into his jacket.

"Mom," a voice says from the couch, low and guarded.

Jackson.

Mila pulls back reluctantly, wiping her face with shaking hands. She doesn't let go of Alex completely, one hand still gripping his arm like she's afraid he'll disappear if she does.

Alex turns to Jackson, who's sitting stiffly on the edge of the couch, his arms crossed over his chest. He looks older than Alex remembers. Not in years, but in the way he holds himself. He's tense and guarded, like someone who's had to grow up too fast.

"Hey, bud," Alex says softly.

Jackson doesn't respond right away. His eyes dart to Mila, then back to Alex, as though he's trying to decide how he's supposed to feel.

"You're alive," Jackson says finally, his tone flat.

"Don't sound so thrilled about it."

For a long moment, Jackson just stares at him. Then, without warning, he stands up, takes a single step toward Alex, and hugs him.

Alex barely has time to react before Jackson pulls back, his arms falling to his sides. "You were gone," Jackson says quietly, his voice shaking just enough to betray how much it hurt. "You just left."

Alex nods. "I know. And I'm sorry."

Jackson looks away, his hands curling into fists at his sides. "You didn't even tell us. You just—" He cuts himself off, shaking his head. "Do you even know what it's been like for us? Do you have any clue what your selfish crap did to Mom?"

"Jackson," Mila says softly, placing a hand on his shoulder.

"No, it's okay," Alex says. "He's right. I should've told you everything. I should've...done a lot of things differently." He looks at Jackson. "But I didn't leave because I wanted to. I left to protect you. To try and give you a better future."

Jackson finally looks up. "Well, that's great, Dad. But what now? Are we just supposed to hide forever and hope they don't recognize you?"

"We're not hiding; we're fighting. And I was hoping we'd all be on the same team."

Jackson doesn't answer immediately, but his gaze lingers on Alex longer than before. There's hesitation, frustration...but maybe understanding too.

As the room settles into an uneasy silence, Alex's eyes land on a small table near the couch, cluttered with a battered tablet, tangled wires, and an old external drive.

"What's all this?" Alex asks, nodding toward the mess.

Jackson glances at the pile briefly before shrugging. "Been trying to see what happened after the broadcast."

Alex frowns, stepping closer. "And?"

Jackson exhales, rubbing his temple. "It got out, but it didn't hit everyone at once. UmbraCorp shut down public feeds faster than I thought."

Alex stiffens. "So it failed?"

"No." Jackson shakes his head. "It's still spreading. Just not the way you'd expect." He taps on the tablet, pulling up an encrypted channel. The screen flickers, showing dozens of short, shaky videos uploaded from different locations.

Alex leans in as the feeds load, each one a window into the world outside. In one sector, security drones malfunction and crash into the streets, their feeds hijacked. In another, a blacked-out government terminal flickers back to life, showing a looping clip of Klepton's speech. A nighttime market—people huddled around an old screen as the broadcast plays, their faces flickering with realization.

Alex swallows hard. This is the aftermath.

Mila places a hand on Alex's arm. "We've been watching since we got here," she says softly. "People are seeing it. Talking about it."

"The system won't collapse overnight," Jackson says. "But it's cracking."

Alex barely has time to absorb it before the door creaks open again. His body becomes rigid, and his muscles tense automatically.

Then Casey's voice cuts through. "Well," she says, stepping inside, "they can't hide now."

She's followed by Talia and Sarah. They look worn and bloodied but determined, the grime of the last mission still streaking their clothes.

Casey eyes Alex, then Jackson, then the scattered tech on the table. "What's this?"

Jackson barely looks up. "Feeds from the outside."

Casey raises an eyebrow. "And?"

Jackson keeps scrolling. "Some terminals are still hijacked. The more people see it, the more they'll talk." He glances at Alex. "It's not over."

Casey smirks slightly and flashes an approving wink in Alex's direction. "Good. I'm getting the feeling we'll need every edge we can get."

She drops onto the arm of the couch, arms crossed. Talia pulls up a chair. They both look exhausted.

Nobody says it out loud, but the enormity of what's happening is palpable. Alex sees it now. Mila, Jackson, Casey, all of them. This fight isn't just his anymore.

It never was.

Chapter 20

Word of Mouth

Jackson scrolls through the battered tablet's screen, his eyes darting over lines of encrypted messages.

Casey leans over his shoulder, arms crossed. She's been watching him for nearly an hour, her expression shifting between skepticism and what looks suspiciously like resignation. "You're sure about this?"

Jackson doesn't look up. His fingers move quickly, tightening the screws on the exposed casing before flipping the tablet over. Its scratched screen flickers to life, displaying a tangle of code that even Alex can't make sense of.

"Sure enough," he mutters.

"Enough for what?" Casey presses.

"For us to know it's not over."

Alex steps closer, eyes narrowing at the mess of outdated tech spread across the table—an old smartwatch, an external hard drive, and a mess of wires. It looks like junk, but Jackson has clearly found something important.

"What am I looking at?" Alex finally asks.

Jackson leans back in his chair, brushing a strand of dark hair from his forehead. "Proof that the broadcast is still moving."

He taps the screen, and a map appears, with nodes glowing faintly scattered across the city and beyond.

Alex frowns. "I thought UmbraCorp shut it down?"

Jackson shakes his head. "They tried. But they can't kill everything." He pulls up a list of flagged transmissions. AR glasses in Sector A—receiving fragmented video. Smart contact lenses—showing anti-state graffiti overlays. Hijacked emergency response channels—looping the broadcast. Retrofitted older devices—resistance hackers patching them into a decentralized network.

"Some networks don't go down; old emergency channels, legacy firmware, junk data on forgotten devices. It's all background noise to them."

"...and they don't monitor background noise."

"Look who caught up," Jackson says with a grin.

Casey's eyebrows lift. "You're telling me this whole thing is bouncing between e-readers, ten-year-old smartwatches, and hijacked government servers??"

Jackson shrugs. "Not intentionally. But that's where it's landing."

Alex studies the screen, his mind piecing it together. "So even if they shut down major networks..."

"The message keeps slipping through the cracks." Jackson nods. "And the more people see it, the harder it is to contain."

Casey doesn't respond immediately. She gestures toward the table's largest screen, where real-time footage plays. Security drones are force-crashing into the streets, a blacked-out government terminal flickers back to life, looping the recording, and scattered feeds show protests brewing; people whispering, sharing data, and starting to push back.

Casey exhales, shaking her head. "Voxx Pop started the fire," she says finally. "But it looks like it's spreading on its own."

Jackson doesn't answer, but Alex catches the flicker of pride in his son's expression before he hides it.

***

It's only been a few days since the broadcast went live, but already, its impact is spreading like wildfire. Reports trickle in through Voxx Pop channels, each one more electrifying than the last.

In the quiet of the safe house, Alex listens to Casey read updates aloud, her voice tinged with urgency.

"They're calling it 'The Vanguard Tapes,'" she says, leaning against the edge of the table.

Alex lets out a humorless laugh. "I feel like Zapruder."

Jules, one of the Voxx Pop crew, snorts from the corner. "I saw someone watching it on a vending machine display yesterday. Seriously!"

Casey ignores him, her focus locked on the tablet in her hands. "The footage has hit every major city on the grid. People are sharing it on AR glasses, smart lenses, and even old music players. Anything with a screen."

She pauses, scrolling. "Protests have already started in six sectors. Mostly peaceful, but..." She shakes her head. "It's building. Slowly but surely."

Alex exhales, fingers drumming absently against his leg. He wants to feel relief—victory, even—but the knot in his chest hasn't loosened since the broadcast began. He knows what's coming.

Casey keeps reading. "There's footage from North Arcadia. Tear gas. Conformity Corps in riot gear. People aren't backing down, though."

She sets the tablet down and looks at Alex. "It's working. You realize that, right? They can't ignore this anymore."

Alex doesn't respond. He stares at the floor, his thoughts spiraling.

The truth is out, but the truth isn't simple. Not for everyone.

Alex hears the arguments in every broadcast clip Casey plays, in every whispered conversation that filters through the safe house.

"They're just trying to scare us," one man shouts in a video. He's standing on a street corner, his face flushed with anger. "You think UmbraCorp would really do something like this? It's an AI-generated deepfake."

In another clip, a woman pleads with a crowd, her voice trembling. "It doesn't matter if it's true. What are we supposed to do, huh? Fight them? They'll kill us!"

Families are turning on each other. Friends, too.

Governments thrive on division.

Casey plays one last clip. It's blurry, the camera shaking as someone films from behind a barricade, but in the distance, a drone descends, its sensors glowing red. The crowd scatters, but not before a young man is dragged forward by someone else, a family member, maybe.

"He was with them!" the person yells, pointing. "He's one of them!"

Alex stares at the screen, pulse hammering. It's not just the violence, not just the fear. It's how familiar it feels.

"This is just the beginning," Casey says quietly. "It's going to get worse before it gets better."

***

The meeting takes place in the safe house's back room, where the air is thick with the scent of sweat, old coffee, and a tension that no one wants to name. The walls are bare except for a single map pinned near the doorway, its edges curling from age.

Casey stands at the center of the room, one foot propped up on a chair, her arms folded. "We can't just sit on this," she says. "We have an opening, but if we don't use it, they will bury us before we get another."

Jules leans against the table. "You mean destroy more?"

Casey shakes her head. "No. We're not here to tear everything down. We're here to build something better."

The room shifts as people exchange glances, some uncertain, some resolute. Alex listens, his mind wandering between the destruction outside and the possibility Casey is talking about.

"We take control of key infrastructure," Casey continues. "Factories, supply chains, financial networks. The things that actually keep this world running."

There's a scoff from the corner. "And what? We start our own version of dystopia?"

"No," Alex says, stepping forward before Casey can answer. "We create something they can't take back."

The words settle over the room. Casey nods. "If we don't, they will. That's the difference."

Lani, one of the newer recruits, crosses her arms. "So we're just supposed to become them? Seize control, redistribute wealth, decide who gets what?"

Casey's voice stays calm, but there's steel underneath. "That's exactly what they want you to think. That the only choice is their version of control or chaos; that's how they keep people afraid of change."

Lani doesn't argue, but her jaw is tight.

"We don't destroy," Casey says again. "We take what they built and turn it into something real. Jobs that don't feed their machine. Supply chains that aren't built on manipulation. A financial system that doesn't crush people under it. At first? It's just survival. But then we make it more. We make it better."

There's a moment of silence before Jules nods slowly. "You think we're smart enough to pull that off?"

Casey looks around the room with a slight smile. "Honestly...I don't know. But after Nicholas, Marcus, and everyone else who fell? We've gotta be dumb enough to try."

The room doesn't quite relax, but something settles. A decision is made, even if no one says it out loud.

Alex watches Casey roll her shoulders, exhausted but standing firm.

***

Deep into the night, in the quiet of the main room, Alex sits with Mila and Jackson. The protests have started dying down for the night, but they'll start again in the morning. The tension hasn't left the air—it's just waiting, stretching itself thin before the next snap.

Jackson is still at the table, tinkering with something. Nothing urgent, just something to keep his hands busy. Mila sits beside Alex, her body leaning lightly against his, her fingers tracing absent patterns along the fabric of his sleeve. It's the first moment of stillness they've had since all of this started.

"This almost feels normal."

Alex doesn't answer right away. He doesn't want to say it, but he knows normal isn't coming back.

Casey walks in. "Hope you all enjoyed this little break," she says, her tone dry. "Because it won't last."

Mila straightens beside Alex. "What do you mean?"

Casey crosses her arms. "You think the elites are just going to fold? You think they'll say, 'Well, guess we lost, time to let the people have their freedom'?" She scoffs.

Alex shakes his head. "No way. They're going to hit back as hard as they can."

"They already have," Casey says. "It's just the beginning."

From outside, there's a sudden burst of mechanical whirring—distant but getting closer.

Alex moves first, stepping toward the window. A news drone hovers over the rooftops, its side screen flickering. Then—

ALERT: UMBRACORP DECLARES MARTIAL LAW.

He turns back to the room. No one speaks.

Casey shakes her head. "Well. There it is."

Alex looks at Mila, then Jackson. He doesn't have to say anything. The war just changed.

Chapter 21

Heads or Tails

The morning after the news drone announced martial law, Casey is already on the move. She's in the kitchen, strapping a knife to her ankle while the others sit, still groggy and trying to process what's coming next. The safe house feels different today, almost like the walls aren't quite as solid as they were yesterday.

Alex watches her buckle her vest, the tension in his chest knotting tighter. "Where could you possibly be going?"

Casey doesn't look up. "There's a backup safe house in Sector Nine," she says, adjusting the strap across her chest. "An old network hub we repurposed a while back. It was supposed to be for this exact scenario."

"And you didn't think to mention it before?"

"Honestly? I didn't think we'd need it this soon."

There's something unspoken in her tone, something Alex doesn't like. She's not just checking in; she's taking stock of what's left.

Alex pushes off his chair. "Let me grab my jacket, then. You shouldn't go alone."

Casey laughs, shaking her head. "Umm...have you met me? I'll be fine."

"You don't know that. It's different out there."

Casey's voice softens slightly. "Look, Alex...if things get bad, you'll know."

Alex wants to argue, but Casey is already grabbing her gear, pulling on her coat, and stepping toward the door.

She stops only once, hand on the doorknob, and looks back at the room. At Alex, at Mila, at Jackson, and the others.

Her smirk fades. "I'll check in by nightfall."

And then she's gone.

***

For a while, the house is quiet. Alex paces. Mila watches the city from the window. Jackson fidgets with a broken tablet, his hands moving more out of habit than purpose.

Nobody says it, but they're all waiting for news. Waiting for Casey to send a message. Waiting for the other shoe to drop.

By midday, the city is suffocating under new restrictions. Mandatory curfews are enforced, checkpoints appear, and the bounty system is expanded. Official broadcasts frame it all as temporary, but everyone knows the truth—emergency powers never expire. Drones fly lower, armed with military-grade rocket-propelled grenade launchers. Checkpoints appear. Bounty hunters aren't just given clearance to shoot on sight; they're getting paid by the government to do so. People are herded into government buildings for "reassessment," a cold, clinical word for what everyone knows is happening inside.

The counter-broadcast plays on a loop on every public screen, advertisement slot, and digital board. President Klepton's smiling face fills the city. His voice is smooth, calm, and surgical in its manipulation.

"My dear citizens."

Not 'people.' Not 'friends.' Citizens.

"There are those among us who wish to see this world burn."

Images flash behind him: fires in the streets, vandalized buildings, people throwing rocks at riot shields.

"They believe they are fighting for freedom. But what they are really fighting for...is chaos."

The footage changes: now it's children crying in the streets and families pulling their loved ones out of burning buildings.

"They don't want peace." Klepton's voice is measured, patient, full of false sympathy. "Quite the opposite: they want anarchy. They want to take from you what we have built together."

The images shift again: a masked Voxx Pop member hurling a Molotov cocktail, a beaten enforcer lying on the ground, a city block covered in smoke.

"And they will not stop," Klepton warns, "until you are afraid to walk your own streets."

A pause. A long, calculated pause. Then he smiles.

"But don't worry. We won't let that happen."

Mila watches from the window, her fingers pressed against the wooden slats covering the glass. "People are going to believe this."

Alex doesn't answer. He already knows they do.

Somewhere outside, a gunshot cracks the air.

***

By dawn, Casey still hasn't come back. The safe house is silent. No one wants to say what they're all thinking. Jackson is at the table, scanning through different frequencies, searching. He doesn't say what he's looking for, but Alex knows.

Then the signal cuts in. The old tablet against the wall flickers, its screen hijacked. A second later, one of the small monitors in the corner does the same.

It takes one second for Alex to understand.

Casey's hideout is being raided. Live.

The footage is grainy, but the brutality is clear. UmbraCorp's enforcers swarm the building, their weapons firing. Figures collapse. One, two, three. No mercy.

The camera angle shifts as the soldiers sweep through the hideout. Gunfire. Screaming. Then a scuffle—fast, brutal, close quarters.

It's Casey. And she is fighting like hell.

Alex can see her for half a second, taking one down with an elbow to the throat. She takes another's gun and fires—one, two—before she's tackled to the ground. She's still kicking, flailing, trying to claw her way free when they grab her by the hair and drag her into the street.

Blood streaks down the side of her face. Her lip is split, and her eye is already swelling shut. But she's still alive.

For now.

Alex releases a breath he didn't realize he was holding.

The announcer's voice cuts through the static. "The traitor Casey West has been captured."

The words make his heart sink even more than the video did. In an age of deepfakes and holograms, words can feel the most...real.

The camera zooms in on her kneeling on the ground, her face lit by the harsh glow of floodlights. She spits blood onto the pavement. Smirks. And even now, she looks fearless.

A deep, mechanical voice overlays the feed. It's not the president; it isn't even a person. It's the voice of The System itself:

"CASEY WEST WILL STAND TRIAL FOR TREASON AGAINST THE WORLD UNION."

Alex knows what that means.

The idea of a justice system is just that—an idea. There will be no trial, and if there is, it'll just be for show. More than likely, it'll be a closed session that leads to a "unanimous guilty verdict" followed by a public execution. Whether they label her an 'accidental casualty' or claim she 'resisted arrest,' the result will be the same. They love to make examples of people like Casey.

This is it. This is the moment they've all been bracing for: the counterattack when the elites are fighting back twice as hard.

Casey knew.

Look, Alex—if things get bad, you'll know.

Now he knows. He just doesn't have a plan yet.

***

The broadcast keeps playing long after the screen goes black. Alex stares at the tablet, his mind running blank. Casey is gone. The woman who pulled him into this fight, who stood in front of a room full of rebels and told them they weren't crazy for wanting something better—gone.

The room feels smaller, the air heavy, as if everyone is already mourning her. No one speaks. No one moves. What is there to say?

Mila finally breaks the silence. "I know I'm stating the obvious here, but she is still alive."

Alex looks at her.

"For another couple of days," Jackson mutters.

The reality of it settles over them: Casey West is a prisoner of the state. And if they don't act fast, she won't be alive long enough to be imprisoned.

Later, when the shock has dulled into a leaden kind of exhaustion, the group gathers for dinner.

The safe house is dimly lit, and the glow from a few scattered lamps makes the space feel even smaller. The two other families staying with them sit at the table, their faces drawn. No one has much of an appetite.

Mila still passes around plates of food; something canned, something dry, but it doesn't matter. At least it gives her something to do.

Conversation is sparse: the broadcasts have stolen most words before they can be spoken.

Then, one of the older men from the other families leans back in his chair. "If things ever go back to normal," he says, "what's the first thing you'll do?"

No one answers at first. Normal feels further away than ever.

The man lets out a quiet laugh. "I think I'd go to the ocean."

His wife nods, rubbing her hands over the worn fabric of her sleeves. "I'd sit outside without looking over my shoulder. And savor every second of it."

A younger woman, no older than Mila, chimes in. "I'd have real coffee. The kind that doesn't taste like it was brewed through a sock."

There's a soft chuckle.

Alex glances across the table and finds Talia staring at her untouched plate. Her knuckles are white from gripping the edge of the table.

"What about you?" Alex asks.

Talia blinks and looks up like she wasn't expecting to be spoken to. For a second, she doesn't answer. Then she huffs softly, shaking her head. "I'd tell her she was right."

Sarah exhales, staring down at her hands. "Yeah," she murmurs. "Me too."

Jackson, who has been silent all night, says, "I'd have a real drink."

Mila doesn't hesitate. She picks up the bottle of wine, pours him a glass, and slides it across the table.

Jackson raises an eyebrow. "You know I'm underage, right?"

Mila shrugs. "I think we're a little past that, don't you?"

This time, the laughter sticks. A quiet, exhausted thing—but real. Someone snorts. Another chuckles. Even Alex feels a smile twitch at the corner of his mouth.

Jackson picks up the glass, hesitating for just a second before lifting it slightly. "To Casey."

The laughter dies, but not the moment.

Talia reaches for her own glass. "To Casey."

They all drink.

And for the first time all day, it doesn't feel like they've already lost.

***

The fire in the safe house's old iron stove has burned down to embers. Most of the group has drifted off to the corners of the house, exhaustion pulling them under.

Alex sits near the window, watching the city beyond the slats of the boarded-up glass. Mila is next to him, tired but awake.

"Do you think she knew?"

Alex doesn't have to ask what she means. "Yeah, she knew."

Mila nods, curling her legs under herself. "Look, I know I didn't know her the way you did, but I can promise you this: she'd want us to keep going."

Alex leans his head back against the wall. "Maybe you did get to know her well because you're mostly right."

"Mostly?"

"She wouldn't want us to keep going. She'd expect it."

A beat of silence.

Then, from somewhere near the back of the house, a voice mutters, "Cut off the head or the tail of this snake—which only strikes when trodden upon. You'll find that both regenerate, as liberty has no beginning or end."

Alex turns. Jules is sitting at the table.

"That's what she said," he murmurs. "Back when this all started."

Alex remembers.

Jules leans forward, elbows on the table. "We need to move before they do."

Mila nods. Alex does, too.

Before anyone can respond, a tablet buzzes against the wooden floor. Jules grabs it, frowns, and turns the screen toward them. The text on the emergency feed is brutal:

PUBLIC TRIAL SET FOR CASEY WEST—EXECUTION IMMINENT.

Alex's stomach knots. A public trial. Not just a quiet, manufactured death behind closed doors but a spectacle. A warning. His hands curl into fists. They're making an example out of her.

Mila exhales sharply. "They want to break everyone who believed in her."

Alex meets Jules' gaze. "Then we move before they can."

Chapter 22

Resurrection

The safe house is restless. Lani sharpens a knife at the kitchen table, the metallic rasp filling the room. Jules leans against the wall, drumming his fingers on a ration tin. Alex stands with Mila near the window, both staring at the same thing—the world outside, where the streets are tense with forced quiet. The city is waiting, holding its breath for Casey's trial.

The tablet pings.

It's barely audible, but the entire room reacts. Jules straightens. Lani stops sharpening. Jackson, already hunched over his pile of scavenged tech, grabs the tablet before anyone else can.

Alex steps toward him. "What is it?"

Jackson doesn't answer right away. His fingers move fast, scanning, decrypting. His brow furrows.

"Encrypted," he mutters. "Give me a second."

Mila leans over his shoulder. "Can you crack it?"

Jackson flicks her a glance. "What kind of question is that?"

A minute later, the message flashes onto the screen—a single line of text followed by a file attachment.

The trial is set for 1500. East Tower - security schematic attached - let freedom ring.

"Well, they're not wasting any time, are they?" Jules whistles low. "That's a good lead..."

Lani crosses her arms. "You think UmbraCorp wouldn't send us something like this on purpose? They know we want to get her out."

Jules frowns. "I was going to finish with, 'or the setup of the century,' so...yeah."

Jackson is still staring at the tablet. "Maybe."

Mila steps in. "Can you trace it?"

Jackson taps his fingers against the side of the device, thinking. "No, not directly. Whoever sent this knows what they're doing."

Jules tilts his head. "So what are we supposed to do? Flip a coin?"

Jackson doesn't answer. He's already moving, pulling apart one of his jury-rigged devices, hands flying across components.

Alex watches, uneasy. "Jackson—"

"Not right now," Jackson says, focused. "I need to think."

Mila gives Alex a small shake of her head. Let him work.

Jackson cross-checks the message against encrypted Voxx Pop channels, running it through different decryption sequences. If it's a setup, they'll have flagged inconsistencies.

Five seconds.

Ten.

Fifteen.

The tablet pings again.

Jackson snaps it up instantly. His eyes flick across the screen, and he exhales sharply. "It's real."

Mila leans in. "Jackson, it's not that I don't have faith in your judgment, but we cannot afford to be wrong about this."

Jackson tilts the screen toward them. A new message has appeared, only two words:

Stay quiet.

Jules lets out a laugh. "How do we even know for sure that wasn't sent under duress? Or the promise of money?"

"We don't," Jackson says.

Lani mutters, "So this is your version of knocking on the front door and seeing if a sniper answers?"

"Pretty much."

But Alex isn't unsettled. He's already thinking, already moving to the table, where the schematic is still waiting.

"It doesn't matter. We hope for the best, prepare for the worst, and make a foolproof plan," he says. "Then we get her the hell out of there."

The tension shifts. Everyone understands what's at stake.

Jules steps forward, rubbing a hand over his face. "Right. So let's talk logistics."

Lani exhales sharply. "If we're really doing this, we need an actual plan. Not just 'hope it's not a trap.'"

Alex nods, eyes scanning the schematic. They need entry points, escape routes, a distraction, and contingencies.

They need to be smarter than they've ever been before.

***

The map of the East Tower is spread across the table, its glowing projection flickering as Talia adjusts the tablet. Every pair of eyes in the room is locked on it.

The schematic shows corridors, security checkpoints, drone routes—everything they need to achieve this. The problem is that it's not enough.

"The trial's happening in the upper court chamber," Talia says, zooming in on the fourteenth floor. "Which means we have thirteen levels of problems before we even get to her."

Lani shakes her head. "Not to mention, the exits are all controlled. If we hit the main transport lines, we're walking into a kill box. Those lines aren't called 'Sniper's Alley' for nothing."

Jules leans forward, rubbing a hand over his face. "All right. Options. Somebody say something smart, please."

Mila crosses her arms, eyes narrowed at the map. "We need a way that doesn't set off alarms before reaching her. Something they won't expect."

"Like teleportation," Jules deadpans. "Talia, you got a magic button for that?"

Talia doesn't even glance up. "Give me a week—and a magic lamp."

Lani asks: "What about going in disguised as guards? We could definitely forge clearance badges."

Alex shakes his head. "They'll be running two-factor ID scans at every checkpoint. Unless you've got a way to rewrite biometric signatures, we're flagged the second we set foot in there."

Jules snaps his fingers. "What about the old press passes trick? Fake journalists, sneak in with the media."

Talia pulls up a list of registered press attendees, browsing the names with a critical eye. "That could work," she mutters. "If I splice new credentials into their database, we could slip into the media pool."

Lani raises an eyebrow. "You saying you can do that?"

Talia finally looks up. "I've already cracked their internal networks once. This is easier."

Jules leans back, smirking. "Okay, smartass. Getting in's the easy part—how the hell are we going to make it out?"

Silence. They all know this is the real problem.

"They'll do body scans," Lani says after a moment. "Even if our names are in the system, if they see weapons—"

"Then we hide them." Mila cuts in. "Smuggle what we can in camera equipment."

Jules nods at the suggestion. "Classic. Who's gonna check the lens bag for a pistol?"

Alex keeps his focus on Casey. "Even if we make it inside, we have to stop the trial from finishing. If they officially convict her, they'll execute her on the spot."

Lani lets out a breath. "We need the distraction of a lifetime."

Talia leans back, thinking. "I can trigger a power glitch in their surveillance grid. Not a full blackout, that would be too obvious, but just enough to cause confusion."

Mila frowns. "What about the evidence? They're going to show doctored footage. How do we stop that?"

Talia doesn't hesitate. "We don't stop it."

Mila and Jules exchange looks. "Excuse me?"

"We don't stop it; they'll be looking for people trying to stop it." Talia leans forward. "We hijack it."

The room is dead silent.

Lani lets out a low whistle. "Damn. That's actually kinda brilliant."

Talia shrugs. "I have my moments."

Alex looks around the room. "This works."

Lani folds her arms. "Yeah, until it doesn't."

Jules grins. "That's every plan."

Alex nods. "Then we make it work. I don't need to remind everyone of this, but I will anyway: Casey's life is in our hands. She looked out for us, trained us, and gave us shelter. She gave us something to believe in; we owe her our best shot."

The group doesn't waste time.

Mila and Lani leave first, disappearing into the city under the cover of the rolling power restrictions UmbraCorp recently implemented—random blackouts designed to keep citizens disoriented and off-balance. They use the confusion to their advantage, blending into the shifting crowds.

Alex doesn't like it. The more UmbraCorp tightens its grip, the more unpredictable things become.

Back at the safe house, Talia is already rewriting the press credentials, fingers flying over the tablet in rapid bursts.

Jules watches over her shoulder, shaking his head. "I can't believe we're betting our lives on the idea that you can out-code an entire global dictatorship."

Talia doesn't even pause. "We're not betting. We're winning."

Jules grins. "That's cute, but if I die because of some typo in your code, I'm haunting your ass."

Talia snorts, still typing. "I don't make typos."

Alex lets them talk. Jules's jokes keep the tension from locking everyone's shoulders into place—but his focus stays on the room, watching the plan unfold.

Mila and Lani aren't back yet.

They'd slipped into the city hours ago under the cover of a rolling blackout, vanishing into the shifting crowds. Now, Alex glances at the door every few minutes, listening for their return.

The tension breaks when the door finally creaks open. Mila and Lani step inside, arms full of folded uniforms, stolen clearance badges, and an old recording device.

Mila sets the equipment on the table. "We've got what we need for the disguises."

But Alex sees it in her face before she says it. Something's wrong.

"Security is way tighter than we expected."

That stops Alex cold. "How tight?"

Lani crosses her arms. "They're locking down more than the trial site. The whole city is shifting."

Mila hesitates. "People are getting pulled into questioning for anything. Suspicious searches. Talking to the wrong people. They're trying to root us out before we even get there."

The room falls silent. They already knew this was dangerous. But now they know it's worse than that. Jules breaks the quiet first, cracking his knuckles.

"So, what I'm hearing is we need to get in and get out before they even know we exist."

Alex nods. "Exactly."

Talia keeps working. "Then I hope you like my backup plan."

Talia adjusts the tablet's projection, bringing up the revised hack.

"Not only will our IDs work, but the system will recognize us as pre-verified," she explains. "That means we won't be flagged for biometric scans unless an officer manually overrides it."

Mila raises an eyebrow. "That's... ambitious."

Talia finally looks up. "So is rescuing someone from the most secure trial site in the world."

Lani leans against the wall, arms crossed. "Still, we need a failsafe. If they override the credentials, what's plan B?"

Jules smirks. "We run like hell."

Mila ignores him, looking at Alex. "We need disguises that can be abandoned. Something that lets us disappear into a crowd the second things go south."

Lani nods. "Agreed. If we have to change plans mid-mission, we need to vanish, not just escape."

Alex thinks fast, then turns to Talia. "Can you rig the press database to make us look like reporters from competing networks?"

Talia pauses, considering. "You're thinking...what? If they flag one of us, we create a public fight to keep attention off the others?"

Alex nods. "The guards expect us to be organized. We give them chaos instead."

Jules whistles. "I gotta admit, I like the idea of being an unhinged journalist."

Talia cracks her knuckles and keeps typing. "I'll set up redundancies. If one of our IDs gets manually checked, we can trigger a conflict between two fake networks. Security won't know if we're the problem or if the media is just being...media."

Mila watches her work and then looks at Alex. "This could actually work."

Alex keeps his expression steady, even as the weight of it all settles on his shoulders. "It will."

Chapter 23

Judge, Jury, Executioner

Alex watches the trial unfold through the flickering glow of a stolen surveillance feed. The tablet is propped against a stack of old books, its grainy image casting a cold light across the dim safe house.

Casey's shackles clink softly with each step.

The guards' deliberate slowness in escorting her into the courtroom makes the chains seem louder than they need to be.

The courtroom is enormous, but the air feels tight, the weight of authority pressing down on everyone inside. Rows of spectators sit in silence, hands folded neatly on their laps like they've been coached in how to behave. It wouldn't surprise Alex if they had been.

His stomach twists as he takes in the steel-plated walls and massive black-and-gold banners bearing UmbraCorp's insignia. Above the judge's platform, the words "Order Through Unity" pulse softly on a digital display, their glow subtly intensifying with each beat. Psychological warfare is baked into every detail.

Casey is placed on a small dais at the center of the courtroom, her chair lower than everyone else's. A camera drone hovers near her shoulder, its red light blinking steadily. Not just a trial—a spectacle.

Alex can hear Jules swear softly from across the room.

"She's still got fight in her," Talia murmurs, watching Casey's face on the screen. "She's not giving them anything."

She's right. Casey doesn't slouch. She doesn't lower her eyes. Even with a split lip and a bruise darkening her cheekbone, she meets the room head-on.

Alex forces himself to take a breath. They need to be ready. Watching isn't enough.

***

Somewhere deep in the city, Alex Vanguard adjusts the collar of his stolen press badge in the reflection of a cracked mirror. His face stares back at him, a little thinner, a little more hollowed out than it was six months ago. He doesn't recognize himself, but maybe that's good.

The man who started this rebellion wouldn't have been ready for what comes next.

Mila pulls equipment from a duffel bag. She's already donned her disguise, a plain dark suit paired with polished shoes that make her look like she belongs in a corporate newsroom. She slides a small pistol into a false compartment in her camera bag and zips it shut.

Talia sits cross-legged on the floor with her tablet propped up on her knees, fingers flying across the screen. The glow reflects off her glasses as she mutters something under her breath. A calculation, a warning, or just an intake of breath when the surveillance feed flickers in a way it shouldn't.

"We're ready," Talia says finally, glancing up. Alex sees the tension in her shoulders. "I've hacked into their live feed. If I get the signal from inside, I can hijack it."

Mila straightens, securing the bag's strap over her shoulder. "We're not stopping the trial, right?" she says, glancing at Alex. "We're just making sure the truth gets out?"

Alex. "That's the plan. But if something goes wrong..." He doesn't finish the thought. He doesn't have to. Mila nods her understanding.

They don't have Casey's mind. They can't win this battle in the courtroom. But if she gives them an opening, they'll make sure her words don't die in that courtroom.

***

The trial plays out on the screen in front of Alex. Anton Kessler is an elegant predator. He steps forward with the calculated grace of a man who knows he's already won. His dark suit is perfectly tailored, and his voice is smoother than polished glass. He doesn't raise it; he doesn't need to. Every syllable lands exactly where it's meant to, heavy with meaning and control.

"This is not a trial of one woman's ideals," he begins. "This is a trial of what those ideals cost."

The monitors behind him flicker to life, displaying grainy, discolored footage of riots in the streets. Molotov cocktails explode against armored vehicles. Figures in masks pull down banners bearing the World Union insignia. A man screams, clutching his leg as blood pools beneath him. The scene is chaotic, but none of the perpetrators are clear—just shadows, implied violence.

"This is what happens when we let people like Casey West speak," Kessler says, turning toward the jury. "This is the price of her so-called freedom."

Mila scoffs from beside Alex. "They really aren't even pretending, huh?"

He steps closer to her dais, his hands clasped behind his back. His smile is almost pitying. "Ms. West claims she wants liberty. But I ask you, members of the jury, what does liberty mean when it leads to this?"

Alex leans forward, his fists clenched. Come on, Casey. Make them regret it.

Casey doesn't react. Her expression is neutral. She would know the tactic: a false dilemma neatly wrapped in a bow. Either order or chaos. Nothing in between.

Kessler gestures toward the monitors again, and this time, the screens shift to show a close-up of Casey's face, her mouth open mid-speech. "You want to know what kind of leader Ms. West is? Let her speak for herself."

The soundbite plays: "If we must burn down their world to build our own, then so be it."

Jules exhales sharply from his place in the corner. "They didn't even try to make that one sound natural."

The jury stirs. The audience murmurs. Magistrate Halden's eyes flick toward Casey.

"Would you care to explain those words, Ms. West?" Kessler asks smoothly. "Or do they speak for themselves?"

Casey leans forward slightly, her hands still chained to the table. She lets the silence stretch just long enough to feel uncomfortable.

"They're incomplete," she says finally.

Kessler raises an eyebrow. "Incomplete? Do you deny saying them?"

"Oh, I said them," she replies. "But you cut off the rest of the sentence, didn't you? How convenient."

He smiles slightly. "Enlighten us, then."

Casey tilts her head, locking eyes with him. "I said, 'If we must burn down their world to build our own, then so be it. But only a fool would think fire is the first tool of a revolution.'"

A ripple of unease moves through the jury; not much, but enough.

Kessler's smile remains, but Alex notices the subtle way his posture stiffens. He clearly hadn't expected her to regain control this early—or at all.

He takes a step toward her dais. "Ah, so now we're blaming the editing," he says with condescension. "A convenient excuse in a world as curated as yours, Ms. West. But let's focus on what we know."

The screens flicker, displaying a still image of a bombed-out building, flames licking the edges, and civilians running in the streets. Kessler doesn't even turn to look at it. He doesn't have to. He's practiced this performance a hundred times.

"This was the Arcadia South Market. Before your movement arrived, it was thriving—a cornerstone of our economy. Now, it's a graveyard."

He turns back to the jury, his voice dipping into something insidious. "And who, may I ask, paid for that revolution?"

Casey watches and lets him have his moment. She's a soldier—there are battles, and there are wars. Then, slowly, she tilts her head.

"You're using a pretty obvious appeal to emotion," she says. "Did they teach you that in law school?"

A murmur in the audience. Alex smirks. Kessler's smile doesn't falter, but his eyes darken slightly. "Excuse me?"

"You're presenting a tragedy as evidence of guilt. But you're doing it without proving who's responsible because you assume that correlation equals causation, that because a tragedy happened, I must have caused it. And you hope that showing them fire and screaming will be enough to override basic logic."

Talia exhales. "Damn, she's good."

Kessler tenses.

Casey leans forward, voice calm but cutting.

"Show me proof. Not just images. If you have hard evidence that Voxx Pop was responsible, that should be more than enough to lock me up and throw away the key."

Silence.

Kessler is pacing the courtroom like a predator. He's not arguing facts, he's controlling the narrative.

"I see what you're doing, Ms. West," Kessler says. "You're deflecting, trying to redirect responsibility away from yourself."

He turns, facing the jury like he's letting them in on a private joke. "She's good, isn't she? That's why she's dangerous. People like her make you doubt what you know is true."

Casey raises an eyebrow. "Is that a joke?"

"No, Ms. West, I assure you that I am quite serious."

"That's the biggest straw man I've ever heard. You're misrepresenting my argument, so it's easier to attack."

A quiet chuckle comes from somewhere in the audience. Halden's gaze snaps toward the sound, and the laughter dies instantly. Kessler turns to Halden expectantly, waiting for him to reassert control.

The magistrate clasps his hands. "Ms. West," he says, his voice perfectly neutral, "I would advise you to answer the questions directly."

Casey meets his gaze. "I am, Magistrate."

For the first time, Halden pauses. Just for a fraction of a second, but Alex sees it and leans forward in his chair, his pulse picking up. That moment of hesitation? That's the crack in the foundation.

Halden recovers quickly. When he speaks again, his voice is heavier.

"This trial is not a debate forum," he says. "Your role here is to answer for your actions, not to lecture the court. And this will be your only warning on that matter."

Casey nods slightly. "I see...so, I'm only allowed to answer in ways that make me look guilty?"

Talia exhales sharply beside Alex. "Damn, she's cutting through all of it."

Halden's expression doesn't shift, but there's something dangerous in the way his fingers lace together. "I would advise caution, Ms. West."

Kessler takes advantage of the shift. He pounces on the moment. "You claim to fight for the people," he says, stepping closer. "But the reality is that the people reject you."

The screens behind him shift again—this time displaying interviews, edited news segments, and footage of citizens denouncing Voxx Pop and calling them extremists.

"Listen to them, Ms. West," Kessler continues, gesturing toward the footage. "These are the people you claim to represent. They don't want you."

Alex feels his gut twist. Of course, they would use this. Manufactured support and forced confessions.

Kessler senses the shift, and he presses harder. "The fact is, your cause is already lost; you are not some beacon of hope. You are a cautionary tale. And today, we will ensure the world sees you for what you truly are."

The crowd leans in. Even Halden watches closely, waiting for her response.

Casey closes her eyes for just a second. Then she looks up. "You say the people reject me."

She gestures toward the footage playing behind her. "How many of those people were forced to say those words? How many had their rations threatened? Or their jobs? How many were told they'd never see their families again?"

She locks eyes with the jury again.

"How many of you would dare to disagree with him—right here, right now?"

Silence. She lets the question hang and lets them really feel it. Then, finally, she leans back in her chair.

"The people don't reject me, counselor. They fear what happens if they don't do what you tell them to do."

For the first time all trial, Kessler falters.

It's brief, a momentary lapse, but Casey sees it. Alex sees it.

Chapter 24

Trial by Fire

The courthouse's mirrored facade reflects the restless city—towering buildings, automated checkpoints, and the citizens who move through them with quiet obedience. Armed security drones hover overhead, scanning, recording, and assessing. It's not just about security; it's about reminding people they're being watched.

Alex adjusts the press badge pinned to his jacket. His heart is racing, but his mind is ready, cataloging every variable that could turn this operation into a bloodbath.

The security lines leading into the building move at a mechanical rhythm, perfectly calibrated for control. Thin red beams of biometric scanners sweep over each person's face.

Mila steps up beside him, brushing a strand of dark hair from her cheek. She looks composed, but Alex knows her too well.

"Four snipers on the upper terraces," she whispers, adjusting the strap of her camera bag. "Guards at every exit. Their response time will be fast if this goes sideways."

"It won't go sideways," Alex replies, more for himself than for her.

She doesn't argue.

Across the street, Jules and Lani move through the checkpoint disguised as security officers. Their stolen uniforms fit too well, stiff with authority. Jules walks with the easy stride of someone who has done this before.

Alex keeps his posture neutral as he moves through the security checkpoint, but his mind is already running through the plan.

Talia should be in position by now.

She'd explained it to him before they left: how BOB tracks anomalies and how she'd have to slip past its defenses without setting off alarms. He doesn't understand all of it, but he knows the stakes.

BOB is fast, methodical, and relentless. But Talia is smarter.

His earpiece crackles. "Camera loop running," Talia says. "Security sees what I want them to see. You're clear."

Alex exhales slowly. They're in.

The air inside is too still.

Alex sees it first on the screen. Casey sits in the center of the room, her hands shackled to the interrogation chair. The chain rattles slightly when she shifts, but she does not fidget.

She watches them instead.

Kessler stands with his usual ease, the embodiment of controlled arrogance. The way he glances at her isn't just condescending—it's disinterested. He thinks this is over.

Magistrate Halden, however, watches her carefully. He's not a fool. He doesn't simply follow the script he's been given; he weighs every detail and potential outcome.

The guards strengthen their grip on her shoulders as the final sequence of the trial begins. Her verdict is already decided.

But Casey doesn't need a verdict. She just needs time.

Alex steps forward in the press line, his movements measured. Not too eager, not too slow. The guard barely looks at Alex's badge before nodding him through. Mila follows a second later.

Talia's voice crackles in their earpieces. "Security logs say you're both already inside. System's still buying it."

Alex doesn't reply. He never talks at security checkpoints. He just moves.

Once they're in, Mila peels away from him and heads toward a different corridor to get in position. Her job is simple. When the moment comes, she has to delay the guards long enough for the others to reach Casey.

Alex moves through the press gallery. He adjusts the press badge, scanning the room. Most of the reporters look half-asleep, their attention on their tablets instead of the trial. They think this is just another spectacle.

They don't know how real it's about to get.

The lower levels are silent. Mila should be in position by now.

Alex moves through the dimly lit hallway, past the access doors labeled AUTHORIZED PERSONNEL ONLY.

Two guards flank the secured entrance to the holding cells. Alex walks toward them with purpose. Hesitation gets you shot.

The taller guard eyes his badge. "You're not on today's roster."

Alex sighs like a man who has been through too many bureaucratic nightmares. "Yeah, because your system's been down for twenty minutes," he mutters.

The second guard frowns, checking his wrist display.

Talia's voice in Alex's ear: "Now."

At that exact moment, the hallway lights flicker. The first guard curses, tapping his comms. "Control, we're getting another system disruption in Sector Six."

Alex doesn't wait. He steps past them, flashing his badge.

The second guard rolls his eyes, annoyed. "Hurry up, all right?"

He's in.

***

Alex's earpiece crackles—Talia's voice, tight with urgency. "They know." A chill grips Alex's spine. BOB must have detected the breach before the humans did.

Seconds later, the mechanical voice floods the courthouse, cold and inescapable:

"SECURITY BREACH DETECTED. INITIATING COUNTERMEASURES."

For half a second, nobody moves. Then the room stirs. The jury murmurs, shifting uneasily. The press whispers, turning to one another in confusion. They don't know what's happening.

But Alex does. He pushes forward, pressing into the flow of the media crowd while his mind runs ahead, tracking the plan. Mila should be making her move right now.

A gunshot rips through the chamber. A guard drops. Screams erupt from the press gallery. Chaos detonates through the room. Alex doesn't look back. He already knows. Mila had no choice.

Guards move fast—too fast.

From the corner of his eye, he sees one breaking toward Casey. Gun drawn.

Then another shot. Another guard drops. Alex doesn't have time to think about it. He doesn't check to see if Mila is okay.

Guards are pouring into the lower security halls. Jules and Lani are beside him, already engaged.

Casey is still shackled. If she can't move, the entire plan dies here.

Alex grips the stolen security badge in his pocket, shoving through the dispersing reporters. His comm crackles again—Talia's voice: "They're locking you in. Seconds, Alex. You need to move."

Alex moves. Below, the lower corridors erupt. Guards flood the security levels, hear the gunfire, and respond. Alex ducks into cover, pulling his sidearm.

Gunfire rakes across the steel-panel walls. The walls should be soundproofed—but nothing is silent when it's this close. Lani drops a guard with two quick shots. Jules shoves Alex behind a column.

"This is going great," Jules mutters, reloading. "Truly excellent."

Alex clenches his jaw. They're too close to fail now. Casey's above them. They just have to break through. His comm crackles—Talia again.

"Alex, we're out of time. BOB is reconfiguring the entire system. You're seconds from being locked in."

"Shut it down."

"Shut what down? It's the whole damn network."

Alex reloads. His breath is controlled. "Then start breaking pieces."

Talia exhales sharply. "Copy. Hitting the power grid. Expect darkness in three... two..."

The lights flicker. Then, blackness. Emergency red strobes flood the courthouse. Drones drop from the ceiling. Alex hears the servos activate, the high-pitched whine of targeting systems coming online.

BOB's voice echoes through every speaker. "Targets Acquired. Initiating countermeasures."

The drones fire.

Jules and Lani dive for cover, bullets sparking off the marble pillars. Alex moves through the chaos, his gun kicking against his shoulder as he returns fire. They have seconds before more reinforcements flood the halls.

Talia's voice crackles over the comms. "I've got a door override coming up. Casey should be—"

A drone locks onto Alex's position. Its weapon system whines, warming up. "Talia, I could use a miracle right now!" Alex shouts, diving for cover.

For a second, nothing happens. The drone jerks and shudders violently, its targeting system glitching out. And then it drops to the floor, lifeless.

Talia's voice crackles through the comms. "You're welcome."

Alex exhales hard. Somewhere above, a door clicks open, and a figure appears.

Casey. Her hands are free, her lip is split, and her temple is bruised, but she's running full tilt. She's holding a gun tight in her grip.

Alex sees the moment she locks eyes with him.

And then—

BOB arrives.

A towering black-armored enforcer, its head a smooth, featureless visor, drops into the corridor like a falling guillotine. Its voice is emotionless. Absolute.

"LETHAL FORCE AUTHORIZED."

It fires. The concussion slams Alex into the ground. Jules curses, rolling away as another shot rips through a pillar. Lani goes down, clutching her side. Alex's vision blurs. BOB moves toward him, and its heavy footsteps vibrate through the floor. Its chest splits open slightly—revealing a multi-barreled cannon, already charging.

No hesitation. No remorse. BOB always adapts. Always wins. Everyone's undefeated until they lose, though. A voice cuts through the carnage.

"The Magic 58!" It's Talia over the comms.

And Alex remembers. AI Enforcers don't have weak spots, except for one. A tiny vulnerability at exactly 58 degrees—the one place BOB's armor doesn't fully protect.

Alex grabs the harpoon gun they had stashed earlier. It's one of the resistance's experimental weapons. BOB's visor shifts, analyzing the weapon. He can't do it immediately, as no one's seen one of those in years.

The harpoon launcher kicks against his shoulder, but his focus is locked on the digital targeting display. It's a simple angle gauge, shifting with his aim. 56 degrees. Too low. 59 degrees. Too high. A breath in. A breath out.

58.

Alex fires. The harpoon launches through the air and pierces straight through BOB's neck with a horrific screech of warping metal. BOB stumbles as sparks burst from its core. It tries to move, but something is different. Its entire framework spasms, short-circuiting.

Talia's voice rings in their ears. "It's done. BOB is officially in the past tense."

For a long, breathless second, no one moves. Alex is barely processing it. BOB staggers once, then collapses dead.

A breathless silence overtakes everyone as they all process it at varying speeds and frequencies.

Jules blinks. "YES!"

Lani, still holding her side, laughs so hard she almost cries. "Magic 58, huh?"

Talia mutters, "Told you it'd work."

Alex lowers his weapon as he sees Casey step forward, staring down at the fallen enforcer.

Her voice is quiet. "We won."

Chapter 25

One for the People

The streets are too quiet. Alex stands near the doorway of what used to be an old factory office, and one hand braced against the worn frame. The safe house—no, it's not a safe house anymore—their community hums with nervous energy behind him. When they found it, it had been little more than a ruin, walls stripped bare, ceilings leaking, and the power grid barely functional.

Now, it's something else entirely.

The halls are filled with movement, voices urgent but not panicked. The old storage room is now a war room, with tables covered in maps, radio equipment, and tablets displaying live feeds from every sector of the city. People filter in and out, some bruised, some covered in dust, all running on fumes. Someone hands Alex a bottle of water as they pass, and he takes it without thinking.

The screens on the far wall flicker, broadcasting the silence. No orders. No mandates. Nothing from the World Union. For the first time in decades, the government has nothing to say.

Alex exhales, his grip tightening on the bottle. He doesn't know what to do with silence. It feels unnatural, like the moment before a storm or the breath before a gunshot.

Then, the flickering starts.

It's subtle at first, a distortion in the bright, sterile glow of the commercial district billboards. Then, the signal breaks—across every government-controlled feed, every embedded smart display, and every neural-linked device.

The truth floods in.

A conversation. Men in tailored suits, laughing over whiskey in a room gilded with wealth. One of them—Charles Klepton himself—leans back and smirks as he says, "They don't want freedom. They want distractions."

Alex stiffens. Someone in the room curses. More footage rolls: ration distribution quotas deliberately manipulated to keep the population submissive. The fine print flashes across the screen: HIGHER COMPLIANCE = HIGHER RATIONS.

The truth was always there, just beneath the surface. Now everyone can see it.

Mila steps up beside him, watching with arms crossed. Her expression is unreadable, but her fingers tap lightly against her elbow, betraying her restlessness. She needs this to mean something. They all do.

Jackson sits on the floor near the radio equipment, his back against the desk, tablet balanced on his knees. His face is illuminated by the glow of every new leak, every revelation spilling into the world faster than UmbraCorp can contain it.

The truth isn't just out—it's unstoppable. Alex knows the moment everything changes. It isn't the footage. It isn't the documents. It's the first person who decides they've had enough.

On one of the live feeds, a government drone hovers over a crowd in Valhalla's central district. For years, they've watched from above, tracking faces, monitoring patterns, and recording who lingers too long in restricted areas.

A woman in a rumpled corporate uniform steps forward. She rips off her ID badge and throws it at the drone. Then, she throws a brick.

Alex watches as the impact cracks the drone's sleek black casing. It wobbles, twitches, and then falls. The room is silent as they watch the moment hang in the air.

A man in the crowd grabs a government banner bearing the World Union's sigil. He rips it down. Someone else kicks over a ration kiosk, its automated voice sputtering error messages as food spills onto the pavement.

The dam breaks. Shouts. Footsteps. The sharp crack of another drone falling. The city erupts.

This isn't a rebellion anymore. It's the collapse.

Lani's voice is low. "They're doing it."

No guns. No orders. Just people deciding they're done. The noise in the room rises—radio reports coming in, people shouting updates across the space. It's happening everywhere.

Factory workers walking out en masse. Underground resistance groups emerge from hiding, armed not just with weapons but with purpose. District checkpoints are overwhelmed by sheer numbers. The city isn't waiting for permission.

Alex swallows against the tightness in his chest. He spent so long fighting to survive, keep moving, and protect his family. He never let himself think about what came after.

Now, after is here.

A static-laced voice crackles over the radio. One of their scouts, breathless, half-laughing. "They got Klepton."

Mila straightens. "Where?"

The response is garbled but clear enough. A private compound outside Valhalla. He was holed up, waiting for someone to save him. No one did.

Jackson looks up from his screen, blinking. "Is he—?"

"Alive," the voice confirms. "For now."

Alex doesn't need to see it happen. He knows how this goes. They'll drag him out of his glass tower and make him look at the world he built. They'll demand he answer for it. He doesn't care about Klepton anymore. Let the world decide what to do with the man who ruled it. Alex has work to do.

***

The first time Alex steps back onto the streets of their community, he barely recognizes it. Not because the landscape has changed; the same buildings still stand, the same roads still stretch in winding paths through the city, but for the first time, they feel open. The ever-present surveillance drones no longer cut through the air. The screens that once dictated government mandates are dark, cracked, or repurposed with messages scrawled in paint.

The people, though, are what make it feel different. There is an ease in the way they move, an absence of tension that once weighed on every step and conversation. They walk without looking over their shoulders. They gather in the open without fear of being monitored. The air is thick with conversations—some excited, others cautious, all charged with the undeniable fact that they now hold control over their own lives.

Mila walks beside Alex, her shoulders loose but her gaze sharp, taking in the details with the quiet wariness of someone who isn't quite ready to believe the fight is over. Her hand drifts toward her hip out of habit, only to find it empty; her weapon isn't there anymore. She lets out a breath as if the realization unsettles her.

"It doesn't feel real yet. She scans the people moving through the square. "Like any second, we'll hear the sirens again, and all of this will disappear."

Alex doesn't respond right away. He knows exactly what she means. The idea of freedom had always been theoretical, something they fought for but had never experienced. Now that it's here, it feels almost fragile, like a dream they might wake from at any moment.

A few feet away, Jules lets out a low whistle as he surveys the area. "No armored patrols. No curfews. No ration checkpoints. Almost don't recognize the place." He lets out a breath that almost sounds like a laugh, shaking his head. "Hell, I might even miss the adrenaline."

Alex glances at him but doesn't smile. "You miss the fight?"

Jules snorts. "Nah. I just don't know what to do with myself now." He gestures at the people gathered ahead. "We spent so much time tearing things down. Guess I never thought about what happens after."

They had spent years dismantling a system of control. Now, in its place, there wasn't a new system waiting to be installed. No leader was stepping up to dictate how things would be rebuilt.

For some, that was unsettling. For others, it was the best part of the victory.

They continue forward, weaving through the streets that had once been choked with security checkpoints. They pass by the remnants of the old world—burned-out transport drones, abandoned government offices, posters bearing the faces of leaders who were now either in chains or missing entirely. The past is still visible, but it no longer dictates the present.

In the central square, a crowd has gathered—not for an official announcement, not because they were ordered to be there, but simply because they wanted to be. Some are discussing logistics—how food should be distributed and how power grids should be maintained. Others share stories from the past few days, still reeling from the reality that they won.

Casey steps forward.

The moment people notice her, the energy in the square changes. Conversations quiet, heads turn, and the murmurs spread.

No one tells them to do it, but they start clapping. It starts with just a few scattered people and then spreads until the entire square is filled with the sound.

Casey doesn't raise her hand for silence. She doesn't make a speech. She simply looks at them and nods once. The applause swells, then fades naturally, replaced by understanding.

The war they fought is over. Now, the real work begins.

In the first few weeks, everything is uncertain. The remnants of the old government still exist in pieces—some infrastructure remains functional, and some institutions refuse to dissolve overnight. There are debates and clashes between those who want order restored quickly and those who refuse to let any form of centralized power rise again.

But amid the uncertainty, one thing becomes clear: people are figuring it out on their own.

Markets spring up in the open, no longer dictated by digital credits or government restrictions. Food is traded freely, not hoarded, for those with the highest social credit scores. Power grids are manually maintained and kept running not by AI oversight but by groups of engineers working together.

Some areas take longer to adapt. There are still sectors where people hesitate, waiting for orders that will never come. But gradually, even they begin to take control of their own futures.

One month after the fall, the streets feel different. There's still destruction—collapsed buildings, remnants of the riots, but there's also creation. Artists paint murals over the old propaganda signs, replacing messages of control with images of hope and remembrance. Musicians gather in the square, playing not for money, but because they can.

Three months after the fall, people have stopped waiting for someone to lead them. They're leading themselves. Schools reopen, not as institutions of state-controlled education but as gathering places where knowledge is shared freely. Science, history, philosophy—people teach because they want to, not because they are assigned to. Once censored and curated to fit a strict narrative, the libraries are now restocked with whatever books people can find.

Six months after the fall, the world is unrecognizable. The old economy is dead, but people have food. They have water. They trade goods, services, and ideas. There are still difficulties—power grids flicker on and off, some areas struggle more than others—but they're figuring it out. Everything is open source now.

For the first time in history, there is no government telling them what to do.

And they're not just surviving. They're thriving.

Epilogue

Engineering Joy

I t hasn't been easy, and it hasn't been painless. The scars of the old regime are still visible in the streets, in the cautious way some people still look over their shoulders, in the ruins of what had once been considered untouchable. But change isn't about erasing the past. It's about moving forward, building something new—not out of obligation, but because they can.

Alex sits at his desk, pen in hand, the ink gliding smoothly over the worn pages of a leather-bound notebook. There's something comforting about handwriting a letter, something tangible that digital communication never replicated.

Mom & Dad,

I hope you're doing okay. It's been a while. It feels strange writing this by hand instead of sending a quick message, but I guess a lot of things feel different now.

The world is different. We fought for something real, and we won. Not perfectly and not without losses, but we won.

I've spent my whole life designing machines, systems, and solutions. It was always about making things more efficient and more precise. But now, for the first time, I'm building something for the sake of happiness. Something that doesn't just function but brings people joy.

It turns out the best engineering isn't about control. It's about freedom.

I love you.

Your son,

Alex

He pauses, tapping the pen against the desk. Outside the window, the streets are alive. People move purposefully, not because an algorithm dictates their schedules, but because they choose to.

In the distance, someone plays music in the square on a real instrument, not an AI-generated soundscape designed for passive consumption. It's raw, imperfect, alive.

Alex closes the notebook, his gaze drifting to the framed photograph of his parents on the shelf. A burst of laughter draws his attention to the kitchen. He stands, stretching his arms before making his way toward the sound.

Mila and Jackson stand at the kitchen counter, the warm scent of garlic and roasting vegetables filling the air. Jackson is stirring a pot with one hand, using the other to fend off Mila as she tries to steal a piece of bread from the cutting board.

"Hey! Hands off, thief!" Jackson nudges her away with his elbow, grinning.

Mila raises an eyebrow, feigning innocence. "What, you think I don't deserve a little tax for supervising?"

Jackson snorts. "Supervising? You've been standing there criticizing my technique for the past ten minutes."

"Constructive feedback," she corrects, swiping a piece of bread anyway.

Alex leans against the doorframe, watching them with a quiet smile. He sees them light, unburdened for the first time in a long time. There are no plans to strategize, no desperate fights to prepare for, no constant weight pressing on their shoulders. They are just living.

This is what they fought for.

"You two done, or should I come back in an hour?" he teases, stepping into the room.

Mila smirks, tossing him a piece of bread. "Depends. You planning on cooking or being a back-seat chef?"

"Neither." Alex pops the bread into his mouth, chewing thoughtfully before grinning. "Actually, I was thinking we should pack our bags."

Jackson pauses mid-stir. "Wait—what?"

Alex shrugs. "We've earned ourselves a little trip."

Mila crosses her arms, eyeing him with amusement. "Oh yeah? And where exactly are we going?"

Jackson tilts his head, intrigued. "And why does this sound suspiciously like you already have a plan?"

Alex shrugs. "Because I do."

Mila folds her arms, amused. "Oh yeah? And where exactly are we going?"

Alex grins. "Why don't we start with some real surfing in Bali and take it from there?"

Jackson blinks, and his entire face lights up. "No way."

Mila chuckles, shaking her head. "I should've known you were planning something."

"Look, we've spent years fighting," Alex says, leaning against the counter. "And we'll keep fighting here and there; that's what families do; they fight out of love. But for once, we get to decide what comes next. So I say we go somewhere just...be."

"Hell, yeah! I'm in." Jackson grins.

Mila shakes her head, but there's something lighter in her expression. "Twist my arm, why don't you? And if I get sunburned, you're carrying my bags."

Alex laughs. "Deal."

***

That night, as the house settles into a comfortable quiet, Alex steps outside onto the small balcony. The sky is darker than it used to be, and the stars are visible again without the artificial glow of government-controlled billboards and advertisements.

He leans on the railing, breathing in the crisp air, listening to the distant sound of the ocean rolling against the shore.

Somewhere, in some hidden part of the world, there are still those who want the old system back. The ones who fled, the ones who still believe power belongs in the hands of a select few.

But for now, they're just ghosts.

For now, this is what victory looks like.

And tomorrow?

Tomorrow, they surf.

Made in the USA
Middletown, DE
21 July 2025

10950891R00128